What Lies Beneath

Count on Me #7

What Lies Beneath (Count On Me #7)
By
Melyssa Winchester

Copyright © 2016 Melyssa Winchester

Cover Image Copyright: Viorel Sima @ Shutterstock
Cover Image Design: Melyssa Winchester

Isabella, my sweet girl. If it wasn't for you, this book, this series, and these characters wouldn't exist. As you grow older and experience all that life has to offer, some of which won't always be the happiest, never give up. Never stop believing in the happy. Just like I'll never stop believing in you. Thank you for being my happy. I love you.

"Dreams don't always have to exist when the suns down and your eyes are closed." — Alex Gaskarth (All Time Low)

Prologue

This is bullshit.

I don't know what I was thinking, believing something that had once upon a time been an outlet for me would still be here.

Still exist.

Better yet, it would still be locked away where the rest of the world couldn't get to it.

The same way I was until Belle crashed her way back into my life three years ago.

Gripping yet another useless box in my arms and turning from the table, I toss it to the ground. Staring without so much as a blink as it hits the ground and topples over, spilling the contents all over the garage floor. Papers, pens and other useless artifacts coming out of hiding and fanning their way out. None of them what I'm after.

None of them the book that for almost eight years, I poured my heart into.

A book that if it hadn't been for Belle doing the same as a kid and me wanting to know what the big deal was, wouldn't exist.

If I hadn't been such a tool back then, maybe I could have found it sooner and the years of torture I put her through could have been prevented.

Should of, could of, and would have. I'm the king of them.

It's been five years since I've seen it for Christ sakes.

Even if by some stroke of luck it still exists and is buried in this colossal mess, there's no telling if it would even be in one piece anymore.

Half the shit in there was written before I could even hold a damn pen right. Let alone the damage that time and weather would have done to it. Neither Dean nor I knew how to take of ourselves, much less anything of value.

Truth is, there's a part of me hoping that if I do come across it, that's exactly what I find.

A notebook in tatters. Thoughts of a messed up kid crumbled and torn and illegible.

The same way I was.

Shit. This bright idea of mine isn't looking so hot now. Tossing box after box searching for the one thing that for years I swore I didn't miss, but the very thing that with Belle saying yes to marrying me, I can't pretend I don't need.

"Look forward." They say.

My mom, Grace, Dillon. Hell, even Belle in the rare times when I bury myself deep in the past and she has to bring me back out. They all say the same thing.

Focus on what comes next, not what came before.

I want to do that.

God, do I want to be able to do that.

I just can't.

Not until I find that book, hand it over and make her see that even when things were at their bleakest, she was there.

Make her understand that she's always been with me.

Right from the beginning.

Ripping the tape off the top of yet another box, one affectionately named *junk*, I push the cardboard flaps back and dive in. Hands meeting paper, I start flicking my way through them. Hissing sharply when after what feels like I've passed hundreds of pages, I manage to puncture my skin.

After all the beatings Dean laid on me growing up, you'd think I'd be used to all the different levels of pain by now, but with the curse words just aching to be spilled, that's not the case at all.

Paper cuts have the ability to bring even the toughest SOB to his knees.

I'm living proof.

Bringing my finger to my lips and sucking away the blood that's managed to push its way up and out through the tiny slit, I finally release the unspoken curses while attempting to stop the flow of blood. Swallowing down the need to say more and pushing the lingering sting out of my head in favor of forcing myself back to work.

It's only when I've finally made it past the old papers, magazines, and even some tattered clothes that I hit what I hope to hell is pay dirt as I brush against the harsh binding of a book. The sting in my finger greeting me as it becomes a full-fledged throb.

The contents of the box that should have been trashed years ago now playing host to droplets of my DNA, but my mind focused as I tighten my grip around the thick notebook.

Pulling it out of the box, I give it a once over before flipping open the worn cover, being met with the barely legible ramblings of my seven year old self. The now familiar racing of my heart as I exerted all of my pent up energy unpacking slowly beginning to fade as I take in the messy scrawl on the page.

Releasing a breath, I pull back from the mess of boxes and head over to Dean's old workbench, throwing my body down onto the thick wooden slats, ready to take in the words on the page.

The more I take in, the further I travel away from the garage and all of its memories. The room becoming drenched in what feels like a heavy fog as I move from the bench to my old bedroom and the bed that I wrote the first entry on.

Back to 2004.

April 10, 2004

She was doing it again.

Belle, I mean.

Instead of playing with me the way our moms want so they can run off into the kitchen, drink coffee and get louder than the monkeys I saw at the zoo last week, she's on the sofa with that stupid pink padded notebook.

A diary, Dean called it.

Something all girls do. *He continued to explain when I asked him about it. Making sure to punch me hard in the stomach when I asked if guys could do it too.*

She's been doing it a lot more lately. All of my attempts at getting her to look at me, let alone smile and laugh, are all down the drain in favor of moving that pen with the pink puff ball on top across the paper.

Making sure to stare me down every time I try and sneak a peek at whatever it is she's putting down.

Wanting to know if it's about me.

What she doesn't know and what I'm never going to tell her, is that I'm jealous of the attention she gives that stupid book.

I want her focus to be on me when I'm with her. The tiny smile that lifts the corner of her mouth up while she's writing...I want it to just be for me.

Three years I can remember coming over here, and after weeks of trying to get her to acknowledge me, I'd finally gotten her to smile.

Well, after I'd failed and made her cry a bunch.

I'm tired of making her cry.

Now that I know what it feels like when she smiles, I just want her to do it again.

Belle is my best friend.

I just wish I was hers.

You know. The way her diary is.

So I'm thinking that maybe, just maybe, if I write in this book every day like she does, someday I will be.

"Kay?"

Shaking myself free of the memory as the soft tone of her voice calls to me, I turn toward her at the exact moment she rests her hand on my shoulder, squeezing gently.

"I called for you a couple of times, but I guess with the all the noise you were making out here you didn't hear me."

Looking away guiltily, I focus my attention on the notebook again, closing the cover and tossing it down onto the bench before turning my attention back to Belle. This time, smiling and getting to my feet when her hand falls away and pulling her straight into an embrace.

"Did you find what you were looking for?" she mumbles against my chest as I bring her closer.

Taking in the mess around me and groaning when I realize the amount of work ahead in order to put everything back the way I'd found it, she laughs, and the vibration of the sound as it escapes, takes me back easily to the first time she did it.

Not three years ago when it rocked my world for the second time, but the real first time.

When we were four.

"I did."

Pulling back, she looks up and meets my eyes. "So now that you've found it, you can tell me what it is, right?"

The calm that came when after searching through god knows how many boxes, I'd found what I was after, is more pronounced now. It's always like this whenever Belle is near. Every beating, every loss, every painful moment I've ever endured, both as the victim and the perpetrator all just seems to fade away until her peace is all I can feel.

Then and now.

Stepping away, I reach over to the bench and pick up the notebook, holding it out between us when I turn back. Watching intently as her fingers run over the cover before coming to rest around the metal bindings.

Her eyes never once leaving mine as I relinquish the hold and she brings it to her chest. The corner resting just over her heart.

All of the scattered pieces of my life strewn about on the floor. What feels like hours spent out here pouring over boxes while sweat beaded and fell down over my face.

It was all leading to this moment.

The moment Belle realizes just how long I've been in love with her.

Just how deeply she'd infiltrated and owned my heart.

"You turned the garage upside down for this?" she questions softly, her eyebrow raising in the cute way it does whenever I do something she doesn't quite get.

Basically, whenever I act like a crazy person.

So, a lot.

"It was important." I explain away with a shrug.

"What's so important about an old notebook?"

Placing my hand over hers, locking our fingers together and being met with the feel of the cool binding as it grazes over my fingertips, I smile as I look from her to it and back again.

"It's not just some old notebook, Belle."

"Then what is it?"

"It's a story. One I wrote when I was a kid…" I trail off, smiling bigger when her eyes widen in surprise. Her knowing as well as I do that writing is the last damn thing in the world I'd ever be known for.

"What's it about?"

Running my free hand over my face and through my hair, the words to explain everything I know is buried deep within those perforated pages completely escaping me, I go with the only answer I can.

"You, Belle. It's a story about you."

Chapter One

Growing up a Walker is basically the equivalent of being raised in a warzone.

You never know from one day to the next if you're even going to make it to the next sunrise, much less the next week, month or even year.

It was living on pins and needles and walking on egg shells right from the word go when it came to the way things were behind closed doors. We always managed to act like the typical family whenever we were out and about, at least until Mom took off and Dean went off the deep end, but behind closed doors, if you went to bed without a bruise it was considered a day well spent.

One of the good ones.

That's not to say it was all bad, because it wasn't. There were these moments when my mom was around in the beginning where things actually felt kind of normal. When Dean was nicer, my Dad wasn't attempting to kill us, and shades of a real family were evident.

You know what I'm getting at, right?

A knock on your door signaling time to get up, and when you do there being breakfast on the table with the milk just waiting to be poured, along with a kiss or two and a smile.

I had moments like that. Just in my house, it was more of a holiday type situation. It was something that if you were a good boy and didn't piss your parents or your brother off to the point where they wanted to lay you out cold, you were rewarded with.

My mom isn't exactly going to win any mother of the year awards, but when she was in it with me, when it was us against the world—before she took off like a bat out of hell—it felt right.

Which is probably why when she took off with some guy from the strip club I've since learned she was working out of, everything changed.

Bitterness, resentment, hatred, all fueled by the Walker anger that my DNA had afforded me thanks to my piece of shit father. I had them all. I lived by them. And in the end, innocent people, some of them who I didn't even know, paid the price for it.

All of this, it's why this book is so important.

Why it's so important that Belle read it.

It's not an excuse for the years I made her life miserable, pushed her away and acted like she wasn't the single most important person in my life at one time. I can't give excuses for that. I know this.

What it is, is a way for her to see that even during those years where I called her names, tripped her in the hall, tortured her along with people I mistakenly thought were my actual friends, she was always there.

The one piece of my history that I wanted to keep safe. Even when I was the one that she needed to be kept safe from.

My time with her when we were kids, minus the times I really didn't understand what the hell was going on with her, I couldn't let my home life taint.

Couldn't let those stupid assholes I called friends at the time destroy.

Backwards thinking, I know. Especially after what happened in our senior year.

What probably never would have happened at all if I hadn't put that damn book in storage three years earlier.

The first entry says it all, and as I watch her curl her legs up on the sofa, her eyes lingering on lines that I know have to be making her feel things, I figure it's only a matter of time before she realizes the same thing I have.

That if I had just kept at what my seven year old self had done, what I had spent years doing, actually finding some measure of comfort in it, maybe I really could have been the best friend I always wanted to be to her.

Look forward.

Those two damn words again.

Niggling at my brain and tapping the way a hammer does on a nail when you're trying to hang a picture. A never ending tap that just gets louder the longer she remains completely silent.

I know I gave her the book to read.

I also know she's got to be given time to do that without me hovering, but I can't help wishing that she would pull her eyes away from the messy scrawl on the page, turn to me and really look at me the way she has in the past. Eyes soft and spilling over with the love I know she has for me. Letting me know in that silent way of hers that everything is okay.

Looking forward was supposed to be easy now that the book is in her possession, but now, as I stand at the corner of the sofa and wait for some kind of sign from her, I'm afraid it's made me do the opposite.

Go back.

Back to the terror, the anger, the sadness and the emptiness that comes when you suffer a loss and don't have the proper tools and coaching in order to cope with it. Back to the nightmare that was my life before that day in the parking lot changed everything.

I haven't succeeded in making my life better. All I've really done is let the demons that we've both spent years trying to let go of, right back in again.

"I still have that journal. The pen too." Belle laughs softly as she closes the notebook and turns to me. "Even when the ink ran out and my mom told me she'd get me another one, I couldn't let it go."

She doesn't realize it, but she's like that with a lot of things. Not just possessions.

If it wasn't for her inability to let go, I wouldn't be standing where I am now. I'm also pretty sure given the status of my life at the time, I wouldn't be standing at all.

Just like Belle couldn't give up on her empty pen, she couldn't give up on me either.

Have I mentioned I'm the luckiest fucking bastard on the planet yet?

Patting the sofa cushion beside her, she releases the tight hold of her legs and lets them fall over the side, curving her body into mine once I've done what she's asked and taken the spot beside her. The feel of her hair brushing across my chest as her head comes to rest over my heart managing to settle the unease inside.

"Did she get you a new one?" I ask, keeping things light even though my brain is screaming at me to ask what it really wants to know.

What she thought about what she just read.

"She did get me a new pen, but the next one was blue and instead of a puff ball, it had a slinky monster thing on the top. Bounced every time I wrote anything down. It bugged me so much."

"Did you tell her?"

"She saw me writing with it once when she came into the room to tell me dinner was ready. Her face lit up like fireworks on Canada Day. So even though I planned on telling her I hated it, I couldn't. She was happy. I wanted to keep her that way for as long as I could."

Another thing she does that even though I don't quite get it, I love about her.

Where I spent years making people miserable and getting some level of sick enjoyment out of it because in the moment it was happening, I felt less empty, Belle was the opposite.

She would do just about anything to make sure the people around her were happy.

A few months after we got together, she'd even tried explaining it to me.

Emotions. Reading them, feeling them, and expressing them, it always came harder to her than it did other people. She says it was all part of her diagnosis. A diagnosis that even after years of being with her, I'm still learning new things about.

But...there I go again, getting off track.

Belle went through a phase where all she wanted to watch were videos about emotions. She would pause, stop and repeat these things for hours. Reading the expressions, learning the facial cues and ticks until it all made sense to her. It was during that period, she had an obsession with happy.

Living with her, I have to say the obsession never really went away. Belle is always better when the world around her— the people even—are happy.

And with the smile she gives when they are, it's safe to say I'm a big fan of happy too.

"So what happened to the pen?"

Shaking her head as she laughs, I catch her eyes and they're dancing. Lighting up just like her earlier firework reference. Whatever happened obviously a good memory.

I love her good memories. They're always so strong they completely demolish all of my bad ones.

"Tristan flushed it and clogged the toilet. God," she takes a breath before laughing again. "It was horrible, but so funny. She wanted to be upset with him, but what was she going to say to a baby? It's not like he would have listened anyway."

Bringing up her younger brother, even if it's a happier memory, makes my stomach twist. Having been there through everything I put her through over the years, even if he might have been too young to understand it all at the time, put a strain on what at first, when Belle and I got together senior year, had looked like a do-over for me in the brother department.

Tristan getting the Kayden that the daily beatings and mistreatment from my own brother Dean couldn't kill.

The better part of me.

What fell apart the night of the dance and that even though we've been on more neutral ground lately, I can still see has a way to go before we can get back to where we were when he was six. The adoration he had for me, the respect, and even love based on the way I was with his sister when he was around.

I miss all of that and I hate that my years of stupidity didn't just damage Belle, but him too.

"He loves you, Kay." Belle, obviously sensing where my mind had gone, says as she brings my hand to her lips and kisses the knuckles softly. "He's just a lot like you. Stubborn and protective."

"I know that, but you're not the only one I've got to make shit up to. I have to do it with him, and I will. But is it wrong that I hate that there's no magic fix?"

"No, but if there's anyone that can fix things, it's you, Kay."

"You're a little bias, don't you think?"

"Maybe a little." She laughs. "But I'm also living proof."

Can't argue with that.

If I could manage to be the boy she knew when we were kids and do things differently with the second chance I was given, then the possibilities really are endless.

I can right all of my wrongs with everyone.

"So..." I trail off, wanting to get into what she read, but now that we're in the moment the words sticking like paste to the roof of my mouth.

"Did you really start writing in this book because you saw me do it?" she jumps in, and after releasing the biggest sigh of relief known to man, I nod.

"For like a week straight we'd come over and you had your nose, hell, your entire face, in that diary. It drove me crazy after a while, especially with the way you used to look at me when I'd hover over your shoulder trying to read. God, I hate that look."

"It's your own fault. A girl's diary is supposed to be private."

"Well, I know that *now*. But at the time, I just wanted your attention to be on me."

"Nice to know some things never change, huh?"

Pinching her in her side, I pull her back when she swats at me and tries to get away, practically crushing her to my chest before leaning my head down into her hair, inhaling deeply before pressing my lips to the top.

"My obsession with wanting your attention is entirely your fault. I'm powerless against it."

"You're crazy."

"Yeah, I am. But only about you."

We're getting off topic, but where I expect it to feel out of sorts, it doesn't. It's nice. Being here with her, the way we've been for years, its right. I don't know what I was thinking, believing that in order for us to move forward to what will one day soon be her taking my name and marrying me, I needed to let her see the past.

Maybe she's right and I *am* crazy.

"What you wrote, what you thought and said…it was wrong, Kay."

"How so?"

Lifting her head from its resting place over my heart and meeting my eyes, she brings her hand up and over my face, cupping my cheek before shifting her body, lifting it until her face is level with mine. Our foreheads brushing against one another with her lips so close, I can feel the warmth from her breath across my face as she speaks.

"You *were* my best friend. My one and only friend. You didn't need to write in a journal in order to get it because you already had it. You had me."

"If I'd written to you that day and asked you if I was your best friend, what would you have written back?"

"The truth. As much of it as I understood at the time anyway."

"Which is what exactly?"

"That I loved you, even then. Maybe not the way I love you now, because it was different when we were kids, but I definitely loved you. Even when I looked through you, cried because of you, or had no reaction at all. I was happier whenever you were there. Inside. Where it counts."

Lowering her hand down until it brushes over where my heart beats a little faster below, she gets her words across loud and clear. She may not have been able to show it in an external way when we were little, but there's no denying that she felt it.

The same way I did.

Inside.

Where the rest of the world and its shit can't touch it.

"Why did you want me to read this so badly, Kay?" she asks after a few seconds of silence pass. "Why now?"

"Our story didn't begin senior year. It began a lot earlier than that. And even though there was a whole lot of years where I didn't exactly show it, before I walk down the aisle and before we start the next chapter of our lives, I needed to fill in the missing parts. I need to show you that even when I acted like you didn't exist, you did. Inside." I repeat her words back, meaning every one. "Where it counts."

"Then I guess now is probably not the best time to say I don't want to read it."

There it is.

I knew it was only a matter of time before she said it. Admitted to not wanting to go back. It was stupid of me to assume she could. After everything she's already had to endure, the last damn thing she should ever have to do is go back. Even if the memories in that book aren't hers at all, but mine.

"I'm sorry, Belle. It was stupid. I just thought that—"

Pressing her lips to mine, she affectively cuts off my words and my train of thought completely until all I can feel is the taste and scent of her as it covers and pulls me in.

Just her.

Always Belle.

"I was just going to tell you to shut up, but since we've both done that before, I figured I'd try something new."

"Why did you want to shut me up?"

"Because when I said I didn't want to read it, I didn't mean that it was wrong that you showed it to me. Wanted to share that part of yourself. I just meant that I *really* didn't want to read it."

Where I thought her words would offer some clarity in the confusion of the moment, it only seems to make it worse.

"Okay, I'm lost. If you don't want to read it, then what do you want?"

"Easy." She bounces back on the sofa, pulling the book from the arm and handing it over with a smile. "I want you to read it *to* me."

She what?

"You said this was a story you wrote when you were a kid, right? And that it was about me. So who better to read it to me than the author? Tell me your story, Kayden."

So after a minute of studying her, looking for any sign that she's only doing what she thinks I might want, and finding nothing but glowing eyes, a bright smile and the overwhelming peacefulness that comes from the love we share, I do what she asks.

I open the book to the second entry and I do it.

I tell her a story.

"Once upon a time, in a land far, far away, there lived this beautiful princess and a beast determined to slay her."

Flinching when her elbow connects hard with my side, I swallow down the urge to drop an F-bomb, turning my attention instead to the laugh that escapes and the eye roll I've earned that quickly follows.

"I'm pretty sure if you're going for accuracy here, Kay, it's the princess that slays the beast."

It was supposed to be a joke, starting off like this. Mainly because I already know what the second entry in the book is about and I'm sweating balls over here worried about how she's going to react when I read it.

Before senior year, nothing about my life was fairy-tale worthy. I guess I just want to keep things light for as long as I can. Exposing myself is the easy part. Exposing my girl to the pits of hell that were the parts without her in it? Not so much.

She's got a point though. She *is* the princess and she *did* slay the beast.

"You're right. How insensitive of me. Let me start again."

As I part my lips to repeat the joke, her finger coming to rest across my lip stops me.

"You're stalling. Which means whatever comes next in this story of yours is probably something that's going to make me cry."

Nailed it.

"Do you read everyone else this well or do you save it all for me?"

Lifting her hand, she waves it before dropping it, flashing me the most adorable smile in the process. She's not the only one with the ability to read people. Like now, without so much as a word, I know she means it can go both ways.

"You're right. This story isn't just about you. It's about me too, and there wasn't a whole lot of good on my end."

"Is this about Dean or your dad?"

Even though I've spent the last couple of years making sporadic visits to the prison in order to see my brother, attempting the same way I did with my mom at letting him in despite everything that's happened between us, he's still a sore subject.

The wounds still as raw as they were when I went through them.

"Most of the memories I can pull up are Dean, but this one, I blocked it out as best I could. It's the one memory I've tried my hardest to forget. It's my dad."

Dad isn't a word I'd use for the man that beat my mother, Dean and me within an inch of our lives every damn chance he got. That name is reserved for a man with a stern hand but softer heart. One that wouldn't dream of putting his hands on a woman or his children in any way other than love.

The kind of man that despite the way I was raised, I hope in the future I can be.

For Belle and our children.

Holy shit.

It's not the first time I've thought about my future, but it is the first time that sitting here with her, with my past damn near burning a hole in my lap, I've been able to picture kids.

Mini versions of ourselves running around. The boys acting like me and creating all kinds of shit, while the girls—who in my mind look exactly like their mother, are lighting up every room they enter. The same way they do our lives.

God, I've got it bad.

"Tell me," Belle prompts, brushing her hand across my cheek and pressing her lips to the side of my head when I lean into the touch. A move so simple that's happened a thousand times before, but that never ceases to soothe me. Like a healing balm to an exposed wound. "If you can't read it, tell me what you remember."

"I'll read it, but it's one of those situations where I shouldn't have even been there. I was in my room, flipping through this comic my mom had picked up on the way home from work and everything was fine. There was a bang, followed by a crash, and all of a sudden I'm not in my room anymore, but the living room. I'm jumping between them, taking what he was obviously about to do to her and wishing I was anywhere but."

My throat is on fire. Acid burning its way through as my stomach revolts against me. The urge to puke getting stronger with every visual of that day I can bring up in my mind.

The day he realized I made an even better punching bag than Dean.

"Kay…" she whispers, leaning her head against mine.

"I'm sorry for this, Belle. I'm so sorry. I didn't want this to touch you. Anyone else, whatever. Never you, though." I say in reply, flipping the book open and turning the page to the entry. Shaking off the nausea building in my stomach and clearing my throat, readying myself for what comes next, I read.

And just like that, I'm seven all over again.

Chapter Two

May 3, 2004

He's angry.

So mad that his entire face goes the color of my red crayons and thick lines pop out on his forehead.

I could hear her screaming, then this crash bang sound, then silence.

The end.

She says I'm supposed to stay in my room when he gets like this, but since she also thinks its okay that he throws her around, I didn't listen.

I went out there.

Listening from my hiding place behind the sofa.

It was like someone pushed a button and stopped time.

It was so quiet.

When things are that quiet, it's scary.

I used to think there was something wrong with my ears when it got like this, so I'd jam my finger in and try to clear the blockage so I could hear again, but since I can hear sounds from Dean's room across the hall, I know it's not me anymore.

It's never been me.

That's when I did something stupid.

I came out of hiding when he raised his fist and stepped toward her. I jumped out and before his fist could make contact, slipped between them.

He hit me.

It hurt.

All of the air came whooshing out and like a piece of paper that blows off and drifts to the ground, I dropped to the floor.

Shadows scare me.

They didn't before. I used to play games with my shadow, but now that I've had his over me, I want to make sure I never go anywhere where I have to see mine again.

Hover. Slap. Growl. Curse. Hit.

He hurt me.

Scared me.

Her cries and the sound of skin on skin break up the silence.

I reach out for her but meet the cold metal leg of the bar instead.

No one can help me.

Spit flies across my face before I feel the sting of his fist in my stomach.

I curl in to try and protect myself, but it's too late.

There's a flood of warmth and it's not from being picked up and taken someplace safe.

This is a different kind of warm. One I know because I've lived it before.

She's done it and I laughed at her when she did.

Belle...

I get it now.

Not being able to breathe, shivering, shaking, and curling myself into the tightest ball I can. It's because I'm afraid. Like Dean says, I've got the fear of God in me.

Except he's not God.

My daddy is the Devil.

I never should have laughed at her when she had an accident.

It isn't funny.

She did it because she's as scared as I am.

When mommy comes back from the hospital, I'm gonna make her take me to their house.

I'm gonna tell Belle that I get it, and I'm sorry.

I'm gonna make sure neither of us feels this scared again.

I swear it.

"I can still smell the blood." I admit shakily. "From where she fell and her head got cut open. Like melted iron or rust. I don't know. I just know it was the sickest thing I've ever smelled."

Admitting this to her, god, even admitting it to myself, turns me inside out. As much as I hate the smell of blood, let alone the sight, I sure went out of my way to make sure it happened repeatedly every day after.

Even at one point craving it like I did air to breathe.

Pull back. You're not that kid anymore. Your air is different now.

My air now sitting beside me.

"I never did tell you I was sorry." I realize, turning and bringing her face level with mine. Running my thumb under her eyes, wiping away the result of her reaction to what she's read.

I *fucking hate* making her cry.

"You have nothing to be sorry for, Kay."

We may have come a long way, her calling me on my crap more than she did in the past, but we're not entirely there yet if she believes even for a second that what she just said is right.

I have *everything* to apologize for.

"She didn't come home for two days and by the time she did, I'd forgotten about it."

"You don't have to explain."

"But I do. I swore it and I didn't follow through."

Swallowing down the guilt I feel for never once telling her I understood what she was going through because I'd lived through it too, I turn my attention to the book and what I know comes next.

More darkness. More torture.

Pain.

"You were seven, Kayden. As much as you wanted to be everything to everyone back then, and I know you did; you couldn't be. It wasn't our time yet."

Pulling my eyes from the book and finding hers as I let her words sink in, I lean in and press my lips to her forehead and think not about the harder parts of what come next, but the easy ones.

The ones that include her.

Us.

The light. The happy. The excitement I put on paper when I made roads with her when we were kids.

I think about Belle.

"I'm still scared."

Jesus. That's not what I wanted to say.

"Of your dad?"

"No." I shake my head vehemently. "I'm over that. I think I am anyway."

"Then what are you scared of?"

"Not being enough. That no matter how hard I try to be different and make things better for you—for us; that I'm still going to fail. Screw it up."

"Well, I guess there's no time like the present to say that I'm scared too."

If I was surprised by what I said, I'm even more taken off guard by what Belle did.

She's afraid of me screwing up too?

"W—what are you scared of?" I manage to choke out, closing my eyes and readying myself for the bomb I just know is coming.

"The future." She admits. "Mine. Yours. Ours. I'm scared of all of it."

"Why?" I ask, even though I'm sure I'm not going to like the answer.

"Open your eyes, Kay. Don't hide from me."

When I make no move to do what she's asked, her hand runs lightly across my face, pausing when she reaches the corner of my eyes and feeling the weight of her own gaze waiting for me to respond, I give in.

I look.

But where I expected to see fear, sadness, or pity, I see nothing but the same things she's been giving me for years now.

Love. Acceptance. Understanding.

Her.

"The future is scary. I think it's that way for everyone. No one knows how the story of their lives is going to play out. We can guess based on the choices we make, but we can never be one hundred percent sure. What I am a hundred percent sure of though, is that as long as my story has you in it, no matter how scary things may get or seem, it's all going to be okay."

"How can you be so sure?"

Placing her hand delicately on top of mine, she lifts it over until its resting on top of the last line of the journal entry I've written. Her eyes meeting mine before lowering straight down to it, intending for mine to follow.

"Because you just swore to me that it would."

Chapter Three

When she said that there was something she wanted to show me and raced off into my old room to find it, I gotta admit, I was curious.

After reading that last entry, despite the talk we had after it, I figured she was going to need a break.

Not that she'd want to keep going.

Add something more to it.

Pulling myself off the sofa at the sound of yet another crash emanating from the room, I make my way across the living room to the hall, calling out as I go.

"What's taking so long?"

When no response comes, I move to the door and twisting the knob, push it open and take in the sight before me.

Belle, on a chair digging through the boxes she'd labelled and stored there, contents flying rapidly from her hands down onto the bed below. Some of it bouncing off before hitting the floor.

The reasons for all the banging I heard crystal clear now.

"Yes!" she exclaims, jumping down off the chair. "Found it!"

Surveying the mess of the room, reminded of how alike we are considering the look of the garage after I was done with it, I smile, which when her eyes meet mine again, she doesn't waste any time returning.

"What exactly is *it*?"

Making her way over, bridging the two or three feet gap between us, she holds a book of her own out in front of her. A book that even though I haven't seen it in years, I know well.

The very book I wrote about when I was seven.

"You weren't kidding about still having it."

"Every single diary, especially the ones with the locks, I still have."

"How many of them are there, exactly?"

"About fifty." She grins. "But most of them are still at my mom's place. I only brought the really important ones with me."

Really important ones.

That must mean that whatever she was writing about at the time when I first started, has to do with me just as much as mine did with her. It's the only thing I can figure given what we were just doing a few minutes ago.

"So what's so important in this diary that you had to tear apart your old room to find it?"

Taking it back from me, she pulls a miniature key on a string from the pocket of her pants and unlocks it, tossing the lock to the bed before handing it back to me, smile still firmly in place.

"Open it and find out."

Moving across the room to the bed, I sit and do as she asks. Keeping my eyes trained on hers until just like before in the living room, she's sitting beside me, her arm coming around my midsection as she leans her head on my shoulder.

"Go on." She says with a squeeze. "Meet seven year old Belle."

"Don't you mean, meet her again?"

"No. I mean, meet her. This is the Belle you didn't know, Kay. The girl filled with the words that at the time, I couldn't say. Words that even though I wished for it, you couldn't hear."

She still doesn't get it.

Belle doesn't get that even though I couldn't hear the words and for a long ass time, I acted like I didn't want to hear them, I did. I heard every word. I've been hearing her every word from the day we met.

"Are you sure about this?"

"To quote Isaac, or maybe Hannibal Lector considering where he stole it from, quid pro quo, Kay. You showed me yours, so it's only fair I show you mine."

There's been a lot of instances over the last couple of years where I've needed to thank Isaac Crawford, and in the end have thanked him. Looks like I've got another to add to the list.

I think I like her quoting movies.

Who am I kidding?

She's Belle. I like everything about her.

"You know...there are much better uses for that quote than us showing each other old journals." I wiggle my eye suggestively.

"Down boy. We can get to that later. For now, we read."

Leveling her with a pout as I sigh heavily, and being rewarded when she slaps my arm, I do as she asks and open the book. My eyes falling to the cursive on the page, neat and steady, but her words from the second I start reading aloud, anything but.

April 10, 2004

Today is the best day ever!!!

My mom got me a new diary and it's even better than the last one because it locks and only I have the key. So whatever I write is for my eyes only.

Then there's the other thing she bought.

I got the art set I wanted!!

Pencil crayons, pastels, crayons and paint. All put together in this super cool pack that snaps closed so little sticky fingers like Tristan's can't use it when I'm not around.

That isn't even the best part.

Wait for it...

Auntie Daphne came over with Kayden, and we painted together!

Oh my gosh! I'm not even done. There is sooooo much more.

Our paintings are on the fridge side by side!

Just like we were when we painted them.

Like we're always gonna be.

Kayden is the bestest friend ever!

He doesn't look at me like I'm weird. Mom does sometimes when she doesn't think I'm paying attention. So do her friends when they come over. It's because I don't talk. I stare a lot and like playing alone mostly.

Unless it's Kayden.

I like playing with him because when things are too much, he's okay just sitting with me. I like it when we just sit together. No words.

It's the best part of my day.

Hang on. He's trying to peek.

Ugh. Boys.

He's gone now.

But seriously, today is the best day ever!

"Wait." I stop reading. "This is..."

I can't even come up with the words. The day I saw her writing in her new diary and was annoyed by it because she wasn't paying attention to me, this is what she was doing.

Writing about me.

I remember that day.

I did everything I could to put days like that out of my head a few years later, but I remember it so clearly it's as though we just lived it. From the moment my mom brought me over and I sat beside her on the sofa bored out of my mind and desperately in need of something to do, right up until the moment she'd run upstairs and come back down with that art set of hers. Two large off-white sheets of paper with her.

The way she dipped her head to the side and motioned to them silently, and me, being clueless and not getting the idea until she'd stuttered out the word paint and pointed to the paper.

God. I can even remember the painting.

Hers of the sky, lines on the page she labelled birds and mine, the opposite.

The water, an ocean, with the ugliest looking fish in it.

Unbelievable.

Maybe wanting to show her my journal wasn't such a bad thing after all. I already had a lot of memories of her from when we were kids, ones I'd tried to bury after my mom took off and I eventually broke away in favor of making new friends.

But now, sharing our thoughts from back then the way we are, we're creating new ones from them.

No matter how bad things got or what she's bound to see the more she reads, this is probably one of the smartest things I've ever done.

"I'm *the bestest*, huh?"

"The very bestest." She says with a grin.

"Why did you want to show me this so bad?"

Slipping the book from my hands and bringing it over into her lap, she flips a couple of pages, smiling nostalgically over whatever it is she's written before turning back to face me and explain.

"You assumed when we were kids that because my attention seemed to be anywhere but on you that I didn't notice you. That you were being ignored the same way you said you were the first time you tried to get my attention at four. I guess after what you just read to me about your dad, I wanted to show you differently. Show you that you did matter. Sometimes, more than anyone else."

I'm torn in two directions with everything I read and she's said.

On the one hand, her excitement, how happy she seemed to be in the entry is infectious and in the moment, I'm right there with her. But on the other hand, this entry and her words serve as a sobering reminder of the hell that I put her through only a few years after this entry was written.

The way I bailed on her and treated her like she didn't matter. Hurt her.

The eight long years I spent that despite the last three, I don't think I'll ever entirely be able to make up for, no matter what she believes about our future.

That's not all, though. I realized something else while going back in time with her through these journals.

I miss the old me. The boy I was.

The one that my mom said would be good for someone like Belle. Well, when she wasn't saying that Walker boys were the devils work anyway.

"How many of these do you have here?"

"Ten or so. Why?"

"Would it be alright if you pulled a few more of them out?"

I don't want to force her hand or make her feel obligated to read her private words from back then, but I'm thinking with as dark as I remember things being growing up, what I know is waiting for me in those journals even though it's been years since I've read them, I'm gonna need a little bit of her to balance it out.

Keep me above the tide.

"Sure. It's not like they're state secrets or something, Kayden. A whole lot of random gibberish with some pretty cool thoughts in between, sure. But not anything I haven't wanted to share with you."

Shifting my body, I move back on the bed, stopping when I feel my back hit the headboard. Leaning forward, I pull a couple of the pillows up, situating them behind my back and when I'm sure I'm comfortable, pat the spot beside me.

"Since we're already here, and here is where I was when I wrote a lot of things, maybe we can do it here?"

Nodding her head, she slips off the bed and heads for the door, turning and lifting up a hand before heading out of the room, the pattering of her socked feet hitting the floor as she heads back into the living room to grab my journal, like music to my ears.

The opposite of the harsher, lead footed sound that used to accompany my father, mother and then Dean as they stomped their way angrily around the house. Belle, with something as simple as the sound of her feet across a carpet taking years of horror and replacing them with happiness.

Creating what should be instead of what was.

After a few seconds of staring up at the ceiling and then taking in the rest of the room, she slips back through the door, but where I expect her to saunter to the bed slowly and slip in beside me, she dives onto the bed in a fit of laughter, crawling across the mattress until she's curling herself around me.

Placing the book of horrors in my lap before reaching up and pressing her lips to my cheek gently.

"I hope this answers your question." She whispers against my face and with a slow nod, I turn my attention to the book. Sucking in yet another breath in preparation of what I'm about to find next. Knowing that whatever the next memory is on the page, it will be as much news to me as it is to her.

As I begin to speak, reciting the date, her next move halts me.

Leaning forward, she places her hands on the paper, a small gasp escaping before she lifts her head, and even though I've seen it happen a million times over the last couple of years, she dazzles me with her smile.

"I remember this!"

Chapter Four

July 10, 2004

I didn't know days could be like this.

When I got up this morning and mom called down the hall telling me to get ready cause we were gonna head over to the Reagan's place, I had no idea that what we'd end up doing would turn out to be so fun.

Weekends always seem to go the same. At least they have for the last couple of weeks.

When she's sure he's gone, she wakes me up and after sliding a bowl of cereal across the bar and letting me wash it down with some orange juice, we go over to see Belle and her mom. Locked up inside while they talk and Belle and I come up with things to do.

Rain does that.

Ruins things.

I don't care what anyone says. There is nothing good about water falling from the sky. At least there never was before.

Today was different.

We actually changed up the routine.

Mom says that we can't do that a lot because Belle doesn't handle it well, but I think that's just something she says so we don't have to go out and do anything fun, because Belle was fine.

She didn't cry, hit her head or have any accidents.

She loved the park!

And even though it's silly, I loved that she loved it.

It's always so hard to get her to smile. And laugh? No way. I should know. I spent months trying to get her to do it a couple of years ago.

Should have just taken her to the park.

Mom found this tree when we got there that was near some flowers, purple ones that Grace called weeds, but that looked nicer than some of the stuff my mom's planted before, and after getting us to eat some lunch, we were allowed to run off and do whatever while they stayed there watching.

I brought my soccer ball, so when Mom said I could go play, I picked it up and went to kick it around. After doing that for a bit, Belle finally got off the blanket, but instead of coming to play with me, ran halfway across the field and straight into a pile of leaves.

Wet, sticky leaves.

It was crazy, but when she came out and was shaking the ones that were stuck to her off, she was laughing.

I tried everything to get her to laugh and nothing ever worked, but give her some leaves and all you hear for miles is her high pitched squeal.

There was this sick feeling in my stomach watching her. I didn't understand it and still don't. She was happy, so I wanted to be happy too, but I wasn't.

I guess my sandwich was bad though, because when I finally made my way over to her, the sick feeling was gone.

Like it never even happened at all.

"You were jealous." Belle interrupts, pulling my attention away from the book. "Kay..."

Okay. I love the softness in her eyes as she's looking at me right now, but I don't have the first clue why she's doing it. Don't even get me started on the way she's saying my name.

She only does that when I do something sweet and unless she's reading something different than what I am, I don't see anything sweet here. Just a bunch of rambling about the day.

"Huh?"

"That sick feeling in your stomach watching me laugh and play. It's because you were jealous."

"Still don't follow."

Placing her finger down on the page, calling my attention to one particular line in what I've already read, it clicks.

I *was* jealous.

Of leaves.

Holy shit.

"Kay," she sighs. "That's so sweet."

"Since when is being a jealous idiot sweet?"

"It usually isn't, but you wanted to be the reason I laughed. It's the exception."

Can't exactly argue with that. She's right. Just like I wanted her smiles and laughter to only be for me when we first got together, I did then.

Some things never change.

Bringing her in close and pressing a kiss to the top of her head, I clear my throat and instead of answering her back, start reading again. Surprised by the amount of words on the page considering how long I spent avoiding writing.

All I remember after that is the chill from the wet leaves as she dumped them on me after pushing me into the pile. Giggling before ripping some of the grass out of the ground and dumping it on top like a cherry on a cake.

She never stopped laughing either. Not even when I told her to stop.

Pretty sure her doing that means my mom doesn't know Belle as well as she thinks she does.

She doesn't know her as well as I do, and now that I know what makes her happiest, I'm gonna make sure we do it again.

Because when Belle is happy, I'm happy too.

"It's true." She quietly says when I finish the entry. Looking up at me before lowering her eyes down to the open book and running her hands over the perforated and bent pages.

The way she looks as she runs her fingers over it, is like she's attempting to commit it all to memory. Like every word I've spoken isn't enough and that if she just delicately runs those soft fingers of hers across the page, she'll absorb it all in. Keep it with her forever.

Like she's already done with me.

"What's true?"

"You loved me. Even then."

"Always, Belle. I've loved you always."

Our story, even at seven years old, was energy in motion.

Slipping my hand over and into hers, waiting the beat that it takes for her eyes to find mine again, I smile when she does and leaning my head against hers, repeat the only words left to say after that entry and what became of it.

"I energy you, Isabelle Walker."

Chapter Five

"What do you remember about Sam?"

There's a name I haven't spoken aloud in years.

Shit. I haven't even thought about him since he moved away when we were eleven.

Yeah, I know that I've got your mind working with that age I mentioned.

My asshole phase.

You know how psychopaths usually start out torturing animals before moving onto unsuspecting people? Well, think of me in those terms and you'll get the idea of exactly who Sam was to me back then.

Thing is, he didn't start out that way.

Sammy, before my mom took off and Dean took over where my old man left off, was one of my favorite people. Second to Belle.

What she couldn't give me, he did.

Playing with Hot Wheels. We had that shit locked down. Kicking the soccer ball around, or heading over to the high school and using their net to play basketball? He was all in there too.

Sam was a small statured kid, but his heart more than made up for it. Quiet like Belle, but without the diagnosis and other random things she did at the time that I didn't quite get, he was the perfect balance to the relationship her and I had at the time.

"Not too much. Just a couple of things that happened when he came over. Why?" Belle asks, placing the plates she'd just pulled down from the cupboard on the bar and meeting my eyes before turning her attention back to the stovetop, where our dinner is waiting in the slow cooker.

"What things specifically?"

"I remember you bringing him over and when he plugged his nose and complained about some smell, you hitting him."

Not exactly the memory I want her to have from back then, but considering how protective I was of her even then, I can't exactly hate that she has it.

Sam, while being quiet, was like a lot of kids in the neighborhood. Especially with things they didn't understand. He also wasn't exactly shy about reacting.

Funny thing is, it wasn't Belle he was smelling that day and I figured that out after I sucker punched him right in the gut.

Whoops.

"What else do you remember?"

"His mom dropping him at your place once and all of us going to the school. I remember you two playing basketball and again, you shoving him to the ground when he beat you."

Tensing at the memory, I take my plate once Belle's finished placing the food out and make my way over to the table.

"Why are you asking me about Sammy, Kay?"

Motioning behind us to the bar where we left the journal when after reading a few of her diary entries, we'd made our way out to put dinner together, she nods.

"You wrote about him." She states and it's my turn to nod before digging into the plate. Thankful to be cramming my now dry mouth with something that doesn't leave a bad taste the way talking about this does.

It's your fault you've got the bad taste. You're the one that brought it up.

Swallowing hard, I wait until her attention is back on me before explaining.

"There was a few months where I didn't write anything. I forgot about the journal entirely. I was so busy with school, then hanging out with you, and the shit happening at home that it just didn't seem important anymore."

"Which has what to do with Sam exactly?"

"That day at the school. I wrote about it."

"Okay…"

"I didn't realize it until I was looking over the journal before we came out here, but the abuse, how I started treating people. It started long before my mom took off. I've spent years blaming her, telling anyone that would listen that I was so horrible because of her leaving, but it wasn't her at all. I was just always bad."

"Kay..." she sighs softly. "You weren't bad. You just had issues and didn't know how to handle them."

"What did I say about making excuses?"

"It's not an excuse. You've spent years owning the things you did. The ways you hurt people. If you were truly bad, you wouldn't have done that. You would still be making excuses or putting the blame on other people. On me."

The way the last two words come out, quieter than the rest, and the way her face is angled back down toward the table, speaks volumes. Unfortunately there's really nothing I can say here because I did blame her.

For so damn long, I made Belle the bane of my existence.

Because you loved her and didn't know how to deal, you big idiot. My inner voice screams, and again, I sit and take it because I can't argue.

"You wanna know why I wanted to show you the journal so bad?" I change the subject and when she perks up, bringing her head level with mine across the table, I know I've got her.

"You mean, besides wanting to share your story?"

"Yeah, besides that."

"Of course I wanna know."

"It wasn't about filling in missing pieces of our story or even showing you how often you were a part of my story, Belle. At least not entirely. It was so that I could rid myself of all the negative stuff that came before. I wanted to make sure that the yes you gave me that day in the park came from the right place."

"Okay, wait." She says, pulling her hand back from mine and just like every time she's pulled away from me in the past, taking a piece of her with me when she does.

I thought I was over that empty ass feeling I get in the pit of my stomach. The one that emanates from my heart when she pulls back.

Guess not.

"You showed me the journal, to what exactly? Sabotage yourself? Make me rethink my answer?"

Is that it? Is that really what I'm trying to do here?

I know I'm still struggling with the person I was and the one that I've become, but in showing her the journal, am I really trying to make her see that side of me because I'm expecting it to change things?

Do I really want her to walk away?

No! My mind screams even before the thought is completely out and where I should feel settled by the way my heart argues so strongly with my head, I'm anything but.

Belle might have a point.

"When are you going to get it, Kay?" she asks, sighing heavily. "You could detail every evil thing you ever did to me, or all the sick details of what you lived through for years with Dean in that journal, and the answer I gave you in the park wouldn't change. The best friend you were to me when we were kids, the so-called monster you think you became and then the man you grew into...I love them all. I'm marrying all of them because they're you. And just in case you're not hearing me, *you* are what I want. Who I love."

Wow.

Way to have your ass handed to you, Walker.

"I do."

"You do what?"

"I do detail things. Sam. The reason I brought him up. It's because it's not just that day on the court that I wrote about. He's there, like you are. Always fucking there."

"There how, Kay?"

"Like a tick I can't get rid of. You being there, the reason for it, I get that. But him? It just doesn't make any sense. I'm not in love with Samuel Hendricks."

"You sure about that? If there's something you need to tell me, you can. I mean, those freckles." She sighs dreamily. "Those were some pretty freckles."

Spitting the forkful of food back down on the plate as the sound of laughter fills the room, I finally release the breath I'd been holding after what I admitted and let her joke do what it was meant to.

Erase the tension altogether.

"I've got an idea." She says after collecting herself.

"Shoot."

"That tick you're talking about. The one that like me, won't seem to let you go. I think I know what it is and what it will take to get rid of it."

"You know what this is?"

"Come on, Kay. It's me. I know everything." She smirks and I resist the urge to get up, grab her and make her pay in the only way I can for her cockiness.

Tickling.

"What is it?" I ask instead and her grin seems to grow even bigger. "Why is Sam on my mind so much when he's been gone for years?"

"Guilt."

"Excuse me?"

"You heard me, Kay. Just like you feel guilty about everything you did to me for those years before we reconnected, you do with him too. All of this, really. It's all about guilt. Where everyone else has seemed to move past it, for whatever reason, you can't."

"And you have a way to relieve me of that?"

Smiling brightly, she nods. "As a matter of fact, I do."

"Which is?"

Pushing her chair back from the table and standing, without so much as a glance back to the full plate of food that she hasn't even gotten the chance to start, she turns to the bar, grabs the journal and tosses it down on the table between us.

"Get it out."

"You want me to read? Now?"

"Yes, but no. What I want is to be able to sit down with my fiancé and enjoy dinner. It just so happens we can't do that until he gets a certain freckle faced, basketball beating boy out of his head."

No way. I gotta make her see that it's not like that. I can put Sam out of my head long enough for us to eat. The reason I brought him up to begin with was because of what I'd figured out while perusing the book earlier and I just wanted to see what she remembered.

And because you're guilty. Can't forget that.

"We can read after."

"No, Kay, we can't. Because you're not the only one that's selfish when it comes to attention. I want yours to be on me, and as long as Sam is in your head, that's not going to happen. I didn't really know how to share when I was a kid, other than the times I did it with you, so consider this another one of those times. I don't want to share you. Especially not with the past."

Chapter Six

July 21, 2005

My head hurts real bad.

I think I popped something in my brain when I was at the court. It's the only thing that makes sense with the harsh thumping it's been doing since I got home.

It's all his fault.

Sammy Hendricks.

What a butthead.

Thinks he's so great just because he distracted me and won.

Too bad he doesn't know that the reason I knocked him to the cement wasn't because he beat me in a game of horse. I don't even care about that stupid game. It's just basketball.

He got shoved because of what he did before he even won and what happened after.

Belle's my best friend. Not his!

She's supposed to hug me like that. Not him!

He's just a stupid smelly kid with splotches all over his face.

A stupid kid that wouldn't stop smiling and waving at her when we were playing.

He's lucky I didn't punch him in his stupid nose.

It's hurting more now. Like I'm being stabbed in the skull.

Maybe I should have punched him.

I like Sammy. I thought he was my friend, but friends don't do that.

They don't focus on girls all the time.

My throat burns. I think I'm gonna be sick.

Why did she hug him like that?

Doesn't she know it was just a stupid game and it doesn't matter who won?

Besides, he always says she smells when he's over at her house with us.

Why would she wanna hug someone who does that?

I tried asking Dean about it after I was done washing off, but he just laughed and rolled his eyes a bunch.

He thinks I'm stupid.

Maybe I am stupid, cause only a stupid person would keep thinking about stuff that makes their head hurt.

But I need to make this make sense.

I need her to hug me like that.

*She's **MY** best friend.*

Not his.

Stupid Sammy.

Stupid Belle.

Stupid Me.

Groaning painfully when I reach the end of the entry, I chance a look over to where Belle sits beside me, afraid of what I'm going to find.

Her smiling down at the book definitely not the reaction I was expecting.

When she looks up and turns into me, throwing her arms around my neck and bringing me in close for what feels like the tightest hug she's ever given me, I'm taken even more by surprise.

Did we just read the same thing?

"Not that I'm complaining, but why are you hugging me?"

"*I need her to hug me like that.*" She repeats the words of my younger self back and I relax into her embrace. "I know you said that you detailed a lot of things and that most of it would probably be hard to hear considering the way things went, but Kay, I swear, all these entries seem to do is make me fall even harder."

Beating up a guy that at one point I considered a friend is making her fall for me?

Again, not complaining. I just don't get it.

"How does hurting someone make you fall for me?"

"It's not what you did. It's *why* you did it." She wastes no time explaining. "I had no idea."

That makes two of us.

"No idea?"

"I was more than just your best friend." she laughs softly. "My mom was right."

"I'm so lost right now."

"We've talked about this before. You remember what she said about the way you used to look at me. I can remember the way it was then, so I knew she was right, but it's not just the way you look at me anymore. It's there in your words too. I wasn't just your best friend. You liked me."

"Of course I did."

"Do you get it now? Why I said I had no idea?"

I do, actually. I also remember what I told her that day in the gym when I recreated homecoming for her. She wasn't supposed to have any idea of my feelings for her.

They were just for me.

"At the time, I'm not even sure I knew what it was that was going on with me. I mean, look at what I wrote. One minute, I'm jealous. The next I'm calling you stupid and making it seem like Sammy getting hurt was your fault. How are you supposed to know, when I didn't?"

"Good point."

"Yeah, sometimes I'm known to have them."

Slapping me playfully on the arm, she snuggles into my side and pulls the book closer between us, flipping pages. Only stopping when she's pushed past about ten entries and landed on the one I warned her about when I'd finally gotten up from the table.

Sam's next appearance.

Three years later.

"Now that we've established how in *loooove* with me you were," she singsongs. "Let's tackle the other elephant in the room."

The reason I'm so twisted up with guilt.

Great.

Locking her fingers in mine and squeezing, knowing exactly what I need in order to get through this, she takes the pressure off when she starts to read.

June 8, 2008

Stupid whiny piece of shit.

Should have known he was gonna go and blab to his parents about what Kevin, Mike and I did to him at the park.

Looks like Sammy really grew into his name. With the way he cried and pissed his fucking pants, he was even more of a girl than Belle.

God. Don't even get me started on that little retard.

I saw her out on the front lawn today, and of course, like every other damn day, the whole front portion of her pants was wet. I don't get it. Why can't she just get off her ass like the rest of us and use the bathroom?

It's like she enjoys sitting in her own filth. It's disgusting.

She's disgusting.

"Stop!" I yell, causing Belle's eyes to fly up from the journal and even though it hasn't happened in forever, her body to shift away from mine as she jumps back fast.

This was a mistake.

Jumping up off the sofa and making a break for it down the hall, my knees barely hit the tiles of the bathroom floor before the bile that's been threatening to spill out since the second she began reading the entry finally expels itself.

My body heaving until there's absolutely nothing left, not even the spit I'd expect after spilling my guts out the way I did. The burn in my throat as I keep heaving only a sliver of what I deserve after what I said about her.

My punishment.

I know I called her names. I know the horrible, sick things I've said about her over the years, but with everything that's happened in the last couple, I thought I was past this. I get all twisted up in knots every time I so much as think about how many times I've actually called her retarded over the years, so this shouldn't have come as a surprise.

Yet here I am on the hard, cold and unforgiving floor of our bathroom feeling just that.

Surprised and twisted in knots, with no sign of relief in sight.

I swore I would never call her that again and there it was, in hard blue ink.

I broke my promise.

"Kayden?" she calls through after knocking lightly three times. "Are you okay?"

"Yeah...Yeah. I'm just great." I mumble before turning my face toward the bowl as another assault takes over and I'm throwing up again.

I am so not great.

"Can I come in?"

How do I explain this? How just seeing one word on a paper caused this? That I hate him. Hate myself.

Jesus.

With as torn up as I am right now, it'll be a miracle if I can even string two words together. I'm not even sure I can look her in the eye after what she just had to speak out loud.

My words.

Not waiting for a response, I hear the click of the door and the sound of her feet padding across as she makes her way in and lowers herself down beside me. Her hand instantly coming out and over mine, wrapping around it tightly.

"Belle..."

"No, Kay. I get it. You don't have to say anything. We can just sit here until it passes."

She's too good for an asshole like me.

She deserves better.

"That word," I manage to choke out and her head just shakes as her grip around my hand gets tighter. "I'm sorry."

"I figured that's what caused this." She motions around us. "You still haven't forgiven yourself."

"I have..." I attempt to argue, but her head shaking again has my fight falling away.

"You haven't, and it's okay. It just means I get to say this again. Say it as many times as it takes until you finally get it. I forgive you, Kay. For the names you called me then *and* what came later. I forgive you."

Shifting across the floor she nuzzles her face into my back, her breath running hot against the back of my neck before she lifts her hands and begins rubbing my back soothingly.

"I forgive you."

"I can't read any more of that entry. I know I said I wanted to deal with it, but Belle, I just can't. I promised you I would make up for everything I did and making you read those words," I pause. "Those fucking names...it's not making things right. It's turning it wrong."

"Did you write a lot back then?"

"A few. Not much. None of it is pretty though. There's probably worse names. I don't want you to go through that again. Once was enough."

Even if it's from me, I will protect her.

"As ugly as it gets, we have to face it, Kayden. Nothing is going to change if you don't. I can handle it. We're not those people anymore."

She's right. I know she is, but it still doesn't make it any easier. Making her read my hatred from back then isn't fair.

"What if I just tell you what I did to Sammy? What we did that day at the park?"

Sighing, I feel her head move against my back as she concedes.

"If that's what you need." She whispers and shifting from my position facing the toilet, I twist around until I'm facing her. Uncomfortable as hell on the floor, but needing to do it more than I need my next breath, I pull her into me and kiss the top of her head lightly.

"All I need is you."

"You've got me, Kay. Forever."

Something about the finality in her tone when she promises me forever has the story spilling out. Every sick and twisted bit.

"Mike stole his mom's smokes. We were gonna head to the park, hang out and smoke a few. At the time, we didn't know we were followed, but then Sammy came out of nowhere and caught me right as I lit one. He started yelling that he was going to tell and the next thing I know, Kevin is pulling back off the tree and tackling him to the ground. Holding him down while Mike and I looked on. I don't even know what made me get off that tree, but I did. I followed Mike over and when he got down on the knees and started going off on him, Kev pulled back enough and I started beating on him. I knew he meant what he said and he was going to end up telling my mom about me smoking. I couldn't let it happen so I wailed on him."

With her hands still stroking my back, she lifts her head up and presses her lips against my dampened cheek. "What happened next?"

"He started crying real hard. Snot pouring out of his nose and everything. Then he pissed himself. Mike started laughing. Kevin too. We all did. I should have stopped then but I was so mad, Belle. I kept hearing him telling my mom, and then Dean kicking my ass for it that I didn't stop. I just kept stomping on him. Dean used to say that as long as I stayed away from the face, I was good. So that's what I did. At some point, Mike and Kev got him up and they went at his face, and I remember pulling back, but it was basically the same as me hitting him. I just stood there laughing while they hurt him."

"His parents called the police." She says and the way it's not a question makes me think she remembers more than she's letting on. I always knew she was aware of all of my secrets, at least when it came to the shit going down at home, but this is proof that it extended a lot further than just what happened there.

She knew just how big of a bully I was to everyone else too.

"Yeah. He ratted us out and the cops showed up. Dean beat the shit out of me with the belt that night. He asked how many times I kicked Sammy and when I told him, he hit me twice as hard with the belt the same amount of times."

Twisting my arm around my back and running it across my spine, remembering the look of fiery rage in my brothers eyes that day after the cops talked to my mom and left, I stop when my fingers brush against where Belle's hand is resting.

"How many times?" she whispers and there's no missing the emotion threatening to spill out as she asks it.

"Thirty-five."

"Kay…"

"No. I deserved it, Belle. God, with how he looked back then, I deserved a lot worse than the lashes and welts I got. I should have burned for what I did to him."

"What you did was wrong, Kay, but responding to that with more violence is worse. What Dean did to you wasn't the right way to handle it."

I don't know if it's her words or my own guilt over what happened with Sammy, but it's like the walls are closing in around us. The bathroom feels even smaller than it is and I'm struggling to breathe.

I need to get out of here before it swallows me whole.

It's even worse because, it's there too. Just like it was then.

The smell of bleach.

Shifting away from Belle, I look toward the door and back behind me. My eyes darting everywhere they can in the few seconds after it hits, just waiting for the moment when Dean is going to jump out and tell me that the only way to disinfect the lashes that are now bleeding is to pour bleach on them.

Fuck, it stings.

Burns.

Scratching at my arms and reaching around to my back again, I start to attack the skin until Belle's hand lands over mine and gently pulls them away.

"Where are you right now, Kay?"

"It hurts."

"What does?"

"The bleach. God. Get it off me. Please."

I feel the wetness on my face before my brain fully registers what's happening and where there had once been warmth, everything has suddenly become deathly cold.

That was it. Her limit. She's gone.

Feeling a pull on my hand, I turn and look toward it and that's when I see her. She's not gone. She's still there, attempting to use what little body weight she has to pull me and all of mine up. Pulling me away from the abyss I just dived into.

"Belle..."

"If your brother wasn't already rotting in prison, I would have half a mind to find him and bury him under it for what he did to you. I never knew. I knew things were bad, Kay, I did. I saw the cops showing up, I saw the marks on you even when you weren't with me anymore, but I didn't know it was that bad. I..." her voice fades out and my brain begins to scream, begging and pleading with her to speak again so that I can find my way out of this.

This fucking nightmare I created.

"I should have done something sooner." She rasps, the familiar delicateness of her tone completely stripped away until there's nothing but emptiness left.

A way I know all too well.

Rising to my feet, slipping my fingers through hers and tightening the hold, I force myself to take control of the situation. The thought of her being pulled into this with me is too much to bear. I need to do what she tried to and get us out of here.

"It's not your fault."

"It's not yours either." She whispers as our eyes meet.

I may not agree with what she's saying, but if it means getting the hell out of this bathroom and the memories that have now overtaken it—overtaken us, I'll say whatever she needs to hear. I can't let her fall any deeper into this. I'm sick enough inside knowing that it touched her at all.

She was never supposed to know any of this.

"I think we've had enough of the journal for one night."

With the slight nod of her head, her body falls into line with mine as I turn and head for the door. The second we make our way through, allowing myself the brief luxury of inhaling the air deeper than I think I ever have before.

What was in my journal. What brought me to the bathroom, and every bit of what happened in there, it has to stay there. I have to lock it away.

Remember her earlier words.

We're not those people anymore.

"Kay?" she asks softly as we near the door to our room. My name on her lips causing me to pause mid step.

"Yeah?"

"Will you do something for me?"

This girl. When is she going to learn that I'll do anything for her? That all she has to do is ask and it's hers?

"Anything."

Slipping her hand out of mine and taking a step back, she closes her eyes, breathing in deep before exhaling and repeating the motion three more times before opening them. Her lips raising softly into a smile as she steps toward me. Her fingers sliding themselves under the ends of my shirt and lifting until working together, we've slipped it off and to the floor.

"Belle, what are you doing?"

Backing up again, she slowly walks in a circle around me, pausing in her second go around when she reaches my back. As her fingers trace all of the lines etched into my skin from the years of it being done, I shiver before tensing.

"What did you want me to do?" I repeat, hoping she'll take the hint and put me out of my misery.

Slipping her hand through mine, she walks us into our bedroom and after closing the door behind us, motions to the bed.

"Sit."

"Why?"

"You'll see. Just please sit for me."

When I do as she asks, she makes her way around the side, the bed dipping in when she climbs on top of it and moves over to where I'm sitting on the edge. Her face angled perfectly with the side of my neck as she places the softest of kisses on my skin, setting it ablaze.

Making me burn the way I did in the bathroom earlier, but for a completely different reason.

There's no rage or hatred behind her touches or behind this burn. It's all desire now.

All Belle.

"Every mark, every indent, and every scar you have. I'm going to kiss them all, Kay. Place my lips over every one and with the kiss, take away all of the pain associated with them so that only the feel of my lips, the love that I have for you, and the trust that we've built, remains."

Closing my eyes as she begins, I fall into her words and let her do what she said.

I let her chase the darkness away.

Chapter Seven

"Are you absolutely sure you want to do this?" Belle asks for the hundredth time since I dropped it on her before breakfast.

"Yeah, baby. It's the only way."

I'm pretty positive it's not the *only* way, but in order for me to be able to move past what happened last night, and from the guilt that's been eating me alive, it's the only way that works for me.

Owning my mistakes is not as hard as I thought it would be. I struggle with it only because I never should have made these mistakes in the first place. I feel bad for every single wrong turn I made. Every person I hurt. Every bit of hell I put them through with my words and physical actions.

It just sucks because you own it, but owning it in words never seems like enough.

It all comes down to what Belle told me before. Actions do speak louder than words, and I'm still struggling with what the right actions are to show that I really regret the things I did.

Sure, saying it won't happen again and living my life in a way that proves it, should be enough, but it never is. Not for me. I want to find a way to make even more of an impact.

Belle says that's what my major in school is about. That my impact is being made in wanting to work with kids like me. The ones that the world seems to forget about. The ones society wants to label and throw under a bus instead of working with for a better outcome.

I think she's right. I just wish it didn't take so damn long for the impact to be made. I want to race toward that end goal instead of baby stepping it the entire way the way it feels like I have been.

It began with Belle three years ago, and now it's going to happen again with Sammy.

Even if it is ten years too late.

"What are you going to do if he slams the door in your face?" Belle asks, leaning back in her chair and bringing her mug of tea to her lips. "Or worse, he doesn't even remember you?"

I've thought about that. Not remembering me would seem like the best possible outcome, but knowing that I'd be making him remember the shit I put him through in an effort to atone for my fucking sins, actually makes it the worst. I'd be bringing up things better left buried.

I'd almost welcome the slam of a door in my face against that.

"If he slams the door in my face, I knock again. I don't stop knocking until I make him hear me out. I actually expect him to do that, Belle. Hell, I expect him to punch me. God knows I deserve it. Whatever his response is, I'll handle it."

Bringing the cup to her lips again, she seems to accept my answer as she takes another swallow before placing it back down onto the bar.

"Kay…I don't want to make anything worse, but last night, something pretty big happened and I think we should probably talk about it before we go."

"I know, and we will, I promise. Just not yet."

"How are you feeling today?" she changes the subject.

"Healed."

I'm pretty blunt with my words. Like, I'll tell you straight up how I'm feeling and not give much thought to the actual words I'm using when I do it. But just like I've done in the past with her, I've done again with just the use of one word.

Her cheeks are heating up and changing shades.

Admitting that what she spent over two hours doing last night helped me heal is getting to her in the best possible way.

Placing a gentle kiss to the side of my face that's desperately in need of shave, she leaves the moment where it is and switches topics.

"So after we get back from visiting Sam, I'm going to love you and leave you."

"Why?"

"Mom called while you were in the shower. She needs someone to look after Tristan."

Well, this is different. It's not exactly the first time Belle has had to watch her brother since she moved in with me, but it is pretty rare. Usually when they're together it's because she's the one wanting time with him and not because her mom needs help.

If there was ever a parent that needed a break, it's definitely Grace Reagan.

Glad she's finally taking it.

"What's going on?"

"She's got a date?"

"Say what?"

"Yeah. That's what I said when she told me." Belle laughs. "It blew my mind."

"That's a good thing, right?"

"A great thing. She's been alone for too long."

We don't really talk about Belle's dad. The same way I am about my own piece of shit father, she seems to be with her old man. It's not a topic that comes up, unless it's in passing. All I know for sure is that my girl made the choice years ago to distance herself from him for everyone's sake and hasn't looked back since.

"Alright, well why don't you just bring him over here when we get back? It's been awhile since he's been over."

"I thought about it, but didn't want to push." She admits softly and her words are like a punch to my gut. No matter what way I look at them, it all comes back on me.

Tristan's lack of trust in me and my episode last night. They're causing her to react in ways she shouldn't have to.

"Belle, if this is about last—"

"It's not."

"You're sure?"

"I'm positive."

"Then bring him over. Unless you just want to spend time alone with him. I'm good either way. You know how I feel about him."

"I do." She agrees. "I also know he feels the same."

Jury is still out on that. I disagree silently. Choosing instead to smile and accept her lips on mine before she busies herself making another tea. This one in her go mug.

Looks like Sammy's not the only one I've got to get on my knees and beg forgiveness from today.

I've gotta figure out how to earn Tristan's too.

✶✶✶✶✶

"Is that him?" Belle asks, tapping me on the shoulder before pointing out the window at the guy crossing the street in front of the car.

Taking him in the closer he gets to the car as he passes and catching the familiar freckles that Belle spoke of when we first got into it, I swallow the lump in my throat and nod.

"Yeah, it's him."

Hearing the pop of the seatbelt as she unclicks, she slips it off her and before I can call out and stop her, she's pushing the door back and stepping out.

Crap.

I was hoping for a few extra minutes to get my shit together, but apparently that was asking too much.

Looks like this is happening now.

Making quick work of the belt, I get out of the car, slamming the door shut right at the moment she calls out to the man now climbing the stairs to head into the house.

"Sammy!"

Watching as the boy I once knew tenses and turns slowly around to face us, I reach out to take her hand, but she slips just out of my reach and makes her way toward him.

"Samuel." I hear him reply evenly when I finally move to catch up. "No one calls me Sammy anymore."

"Oh, I'm sorry. Samuel." Belle apologizes and with that simple move, just like she does with every person she's been around, his shoulders relax and the faintest trace of a smile appears.

"It's alright. I'm sorry. You seem to know my name, but I don't know yours. Do we know each other?"

I could step in right now and take it from here, but before I can so much as get the words straight in my head, Belle is at it again.

"We did." She tells him. "Before. My name is Isabelle."

"Belle?" Samuel asks as recognition dawns in his eyes. All traces of his earlier reaction erased and the soft look I remember him having when we were kids taking its place.

"Yep, and this," she pauses, pointing toward me with the brightest smile. "This is Kayden."

There it is.

The reaction I was expecting.

It's so subtle and quick that I don't think Belle caught it, but the friendliness he may have had toward her is now replaced with something far different. Anger. Upset.

Fear.

Even after all these years and him moving away, my name still sparks a sliver of fear.

This sucks.

"What are you doing here?" He asks, but before either of us can answer, he asks another question and this one is even more expected than the first. "What are you doing here together?"

Seems little Sammy remembers exactly the way things were when he left town and Belle, god love her, is completely oblivious as her cheeks are again changing colors.

"We're together." I finally force out and pulling his attention away from Belle, he meets me head on. His stance hardening at the sound of my voice, but not cowering the way he used to so damn long ago.

Good for him. If anyone should cower, it should be me.

"What are you doing here?" he repeats.

"Making shit right. That is, if you're willing to hear me out."

"Why now?"

"Because my head was jammed too far up my ass back then to do it?" I admit honestly.

If he thinks for a second that I'm going to make excuses for my behavior, he's got another thing coming. Those days are over.

I can't say I had a clue how this was going to go down when I decided I wanted to do it, but him laughing was definitely not part of the equation. Yet standing here now on his front lawn, the moment as tense as ever, that's exactly what's happening.

"Why are you laughing?" Belle asks, pulling the question straight out of my head.

"Well, I had to figure if the two of you were here together, it meant that the shit he said and did to you when we were kids was long since forgiven. Even more so if the two of you are actually dating, which by the way, I called when we were eight. Though, he was too pigheaded to believe me at the time." He laughs again. "But the real reason I laughed is because of all the things I expected him to say to me when we came face to face again, that wasn't it."

Pigheaded. *Check.*

Asshole. *Check.*

Never apologizing for my actions.

What do you know, I'm three for three. He's nailed me—at least the old me—spot on.

"There's no excuse for the shit I did to you, Sam. There's no excuse for the shit I did to anyone back then. I came here figuring I would explain to you what was going on at the time, how fucked up I was and that maybe, you'd see the honesty for yourself and believe me. But on the way over here, I realized that my shitty home life, my anger issues, and the crap I was going through, means absolute shit. I was a dick to you and I was an even bigger one for not owning up to that fact years ago. I'm sorry."

"You *were* a dick. You were even worse with her, as I recall." He shifts his attention away from me and back to Belle. "The thing is, the world is full of dicks, Kayden. And as much as I feared you then, as much as I still may fear you now because of what went down with us, I gotta say, you were good practice."

"Excuse me?"

He can't possibly mean what I think he means.

"I'm saying," he pauses, running his hand down over his face and sighing. "I'm saying I forgive you. I mean, that is what you came here for, isn't it? You want to make things right? Move on from the past?"

There's no way it can be this easy. No way that after the hell I put him through, that he can stand here now and just be over it.

There has got to be a catch.

"Is this where you throw me off by saying that, and kick the shit out of me or something?" I ask and again he laughs, but this time, Belle seems to find it funny too because she joins him.

"No, Kayden. It's the part where I say that we're not kids anymore, and that what you did back then, I'm over it. Sadly, you weren't the worst of it." Pausing, he lifts up his sleeve, and where I expect to see scars, I'm met with something else entirely. His arms are burned. "So, whatever shit you're giving yourself over what happened back then, stop. You're forgiven."

There's something about the way he says I wasn't the worst, along with his seared skin that does me in. I'm not exactly a saint, but ever since I grew a set, changed my ways, and attempted to do better, I've gone out of my way to stop shit like that before it can even start. The memory of Belle and the cigarette burn on her arm as vivid as the day it happened.

Obviously small in comparison to whatever it is that Samuel had to live through after he moved away.

Looking away when I sense Belle moving out of the corner of my eye, I watch as she does the same with her own sleeve, pulling it up just past her wrist to where the scar from her burn still remains. Eyes locked on Sam's, she stands there in quiet solidarity.

Letting him know he's not alone.

"I'm sorry, Belle." He says and she isn't the only one whose eyes go wide in surprise.

What the hell does he have to apologize for?

"Bet you didn't see that coming." He grins before his mouth drops and he's back to serious again. "Kayden's not the only one that acted like an ass when we were kids. I said some pretty awful stuff to you back then too. Assumed things because I was too stupid to understand or ask questions. I'm sorry for that, and sorry that we have this in common."

Looking at his arm and then back to Belle's he slides his sleeve back down and accepts Belle's hug when she steps forward with her arms outstretched.

"You wanna know what you can do to make shit right, Kayden?" He asks when Belle pulls away and steps back over to where I'm standing, sliding her body into mine. "You can take that girl home and continue doing what you have been. Be the guy she always knew was there and just be happy. Spread enough of that shit around and maybe twenty years from now, it won't be our kids repeating history and having this conversation. Think you can do that?"

Looking down at Belle and placing a kiss to the side of her head, I give him what he's after. Only it's not only words I know he wants to hear, but the truth too.

"There's nothing I wanna do more."

"Good. Now, I've got a girl on the other side of that door waiting for this." He motions down to the plastic bag around his arm. "And you know how they say you won't like the Hulk when he's angry? Well that green bastard ain't got nothing on my girl. So, I better get in there."

Chuckling under my breath, I step forward when I see his hand come out and meet him halfway, gripping onto it tight and meeting his eyes. Letting him know without a word being spoken just how thankful I am for what he's given me.

Turning toward the car, ready to let him head inside, I head over and unlock and open my door, about to slide in when I hear him call out.

"Yeah?"

"Next time you wanna pop by, bring a basketball."

"Why?" I laugh at his recollection of the past. "You itching to get beat again?"

As the sound of his laughter filters across the grass, a weight lifts of my shoulders. With that one gesture, I'm finally freed of the burden I've been carrying around for almost ten years.

"Something tells me with the way things turned out, there are no losers here."

"How do you figure?"

"I won the game and you, well, you got the real prize. You got the girl!"

When I see Belle's face light up from her position in the car, I'm left with only one thought as I nod toward him and tap the car before slipping down in beside her.

Sammy is right.

We're all winners.

Chapter Eight

It's been hours since we left Sam's place and came home. Belle has gone across the street, picked up Tristan, and we've cooked and eaten dinner. She's put the dishes in the dishwasher and even set the thing to go, and in all of that time, I still can't get the image of his arms out of my head.

How did he end up being burned after he moved away? What kind of sadistic fucker did he run into that thought burning someone alive was the way to go?

Amelia and the cigarette burns, as wrong as they were, had an origin. It wasn't one any of us knew at the time, though I suspected something was up when we dated and she wore hoodies all the time. None of that even matters though, because at the end of the day, there is someone out there in the next town over from us, who is a hell of a lot worse than Amelia, Dillon or I ever were.

God.

It's like being back in high school all over again. Seeing the mark from the cigarette burning bright red on Belle's skin, and now, years later, an indent in her flesh. A mark that no matter where we go or what we do in life, we'll never be able to entirely escape from.

We'll always remember.

And if the way I'm reacting to Samuel's burns now is any indication, it's also something I'll never be able to forgive myself for either.

You can't save everyone, Kayden. All you can do is what Sam wanted you to. The rest has to be on everyone else.

No matter how many times I've repeated that since we got in the car and pulled away, I can't seem to let it sink in. I want more than anything to go back in time and kick my own head in so I never touched him in the first place.

Never turned into the monster I became.

"Kay? Did you hear what I said?"

Shaking myself out of my thoughts, I turn toward the bar where for the last thirty or so minutes, Belle has been helping Tristan with his math homework.

"No, sorry. What did I miss?"

"Tristan asked if now that we're done, we could all watch a movie together before I have to kick him to bed."

Is she actually asking my permission? Since when do we do that?

"Sure, of course. What kind of movie did you have in mind?"

"Something gory." Tristan says, grinning like a Cheshire cat.

"So basically you wanna watch something your mom told you is off limits?" I ask and with how quickly he shakes his head but can't meet my eyes tells me I've hit my mark.

"Tristan, you know I don't like those kinds of movies." Belle interjects and going back to one of our first conversations and seeing over the years firsthand how she reacts to anything remotely scary, I laugh, causing both of them to stare me down.

"If my vote counts, I say we let him pick one."

"Kayden."

"Belle." I repeat back with a grin.

She doesn't stand a chance. With the smile starting to appear on her brother's face, I'm pretty sure she's losing the fight.

It's officially two on one.

"If you don't wanna watch, you can always read." I offer, reaching over on the sofa and grabbing her Kindle from the arm, shaking it back and forth.

Leveling me with a scowl, I just smile serenely and after a few seconds of trying to maintain the look, she caves like she always does and sighs, motioning down the hall to Tristan.

"Go pick whatever you want. I'll make the popcorn." I tell him, sliding myself up off the sofa and making a beeline for the kitchen just as he jumps off the barstool.

"Hey, Kayden?" he calls back when he hits the door to my old room.

"Yeah?"

"You wanna help me pick?"

Seeing this for the opportunity it is, I don't even hesitate. This is the first time in what feels like forever that he's asking me to do something with him instead of just having his sister force his hand. I'd be stupid not to take it.

"Yeah, buddy. Give me a second with Belle and I'll be right there."

"Gross. You're gonna kiss her again, aren't you?"

"Actually, no. I was going to start the popcorn, but now that you mention it..."

"Eww. Whatever. Just don't take too long."

Dipping into the room, I do the exact thing Tristan called me on and pull Belle into my arms, warmed immediately by the squeal she lets escape before my lips find hers.

"He's knows us too well." Belle laughs against my lips when we finally come up for air.

"He does, but it's not exactly a bad thing. No matter how gross he thinks it is. He's been a part of me doing a lot worse. Witnessing me make up for that by being overly affectionate could be a good thing."

"Or, it could result in him puking all over the carpet." She jokes and I press my lips to hers again, silencing the laughter until it's nothing but a rumble in her chest that quickly manages to morph into a moan.

A moan that even years after she did it for the first time, I never get tired of hearing.

"I better go before he decides he doesn't want my help." I tell her, pressing another delicate kiss to her nose before swatting her on her ass. "You mind starting the popcorn?"

Shooing me away with a roll of her eyes and a crooked smile, I head off toward the room, the light in her eyes and the laughter that comes when I turn and blow her a kiss before ducking inside another reminder of why she's home.

Why I can't imagine my life without her in it.

Looking toward the DVD shelves when I step in, expecting to see Tristan going through them, I come up empty. It's only when I turn toward the bed and take in the book now sitting open in his lap that my heart sinks in my chest.

"Tristan, look...It's not what you think."

He lifts his eyes from the page, but where I expect to see hurt, he's showing me the opposite. He's open.

"You wrote about her."

"Yeah, buddy, I did."

"No, Kayden. You don't get it. You wrote about her and you were *nice*."

I'm sure he doesn't mean to take the knife that now feels like its plunging deep into my chest cavity and twist it as deeply as he is, but it's happening none the less. Because before I made such a colossal mess of things in our senior year, he actually seemed to like me.

Being nice then wouldn't have been the obvious shock it is to him now.

Careful of each step I make, not wanting to ruin the obvious opening I have, I slowly move toward the bed and stop beside him, not making a move to sit until he pats the blanket.

"I wasn't always an asshole, Tris."

"I know."

"You do?"

"Yeah." He admits and the tightness in my chest seeing him reading my old journal begins to ease. "I guess I just forgot for a while because of all the other stuff that happened."

"Tris, what happened back then—"

"No. You don't have to say it. Belle tells me enough as it is. I know it wasn't all your fault. It just wouldn't have happened at all if you stayed around like she wished you did."

"I know."

"You made her cry so much, Kayden. So much. I used to count the nights, you know? After I hit fourteen, I stopped. For a long time, I didn't even realize the person that was making her cry was you because I could remember you from when I was little. You weren't mean. You used to play with me. I *couldn't* believe it was you."

I don't know what to tell him. I could apologize for all of those days I made his sister cry, but I don't think it would fix anything.

It's a lame response for what I did.

"That changed the night of homecoming. I knew then it was you. You broke her."

"Tristan, I know it probably doesn't mean shit, but I need you to hear me. Who I was back then, the things I did...none of that was Belle. It was all me. I know what a mess I was. A mess I made. I hate myself for not changing things sooner. For walking away from her and never looking back. But she's giving me this chance to make things right. To love her the way I should have. The way I always have even when I couldn't admit it to myself. I hope that someday soon, maybe I can earn that same thing from you. I hope I can make it up to you."

"You already have."

Say what?

"I hated you for a long time. A *long* time. All that did was make me sick inside. I know you think I'm just a stupid kid but—"

"Not true." I cut him off. No way in hell am I letting him believe for a second that I've ever seen him that way. It's about damn time he knew the truth. "I think you're my brother, Tristan. You're just my brother."

"Really?"

God. He's got Belle's eyes. It's like I'm looking at the girl from my past all over again.

"Yes, really. I lived with Dean for so long that I actually started to believe that's what a normal sibling relationship was like. Then, there you were. You used to look at me like I was some sort of God. It made me feel special. Then there's the way you and Belle always were together. It wasn't like Dean and I. The complete opposite actually. It made me wish *you* were my brother."

"I can be." He answers softly. "If you want."

"You already are."

"I'm sorry, Kayden."

"No, Tris. Brothers don't do that to each other. It's a rule and I broke it. I'm the one that's sorry. So god damned sorry."

I don't have a lot of experience with hugs outside of my mom and then later on, Belle and her mom, but I'm pretty sure with the way he throws himself into me, this might be the best damn hug I've ever gotten.

There's no thought that goes into it before it's done. It's loose until he's got a grip and then it's tight. Warm. So warm that every part of you is affected by it. Its innocent and real and the longer he holds his position, the longer I want to keep it there.

I've experienced so damn much over the last three years, things that I wouldn't change for anything, but Tristan hugging me now, he's giving me something new. Something that no one else in the world will ever be able to give me.

He's giving me the chance to be a brother. To do it right this time.

"Okay, enough of this." I joke when he pulls back, wiping a hand across my eyes when he lowers his gaze to the book. "Did you pick what you wanted to watch?"

"Did you really go puddle jumping in the rain with Belle when you were my age?" He switches gears.

Looking down at the year on the page, I shake my head. "No. When I was your age, I was...well, I wasn't there. This was a couple of years before that though, and yeah, I did it. Loved it too."

"Do you think you'd like doing it now?"

"Don't know. Haven't had the chance to do it, but can't see why not. Why?"

"The next time it rains, I think we should do it."

"You and me?"

It's his turn to shake his head and the way his hair whips from side to side as he does it makes me remember just how unruly mine used to be when I was his age.

"You, me *and* Belle."

"You got a deal, Tris. But only if you pick two movies and meet me on the sofa in five minutes."

"Why five minutes?" he asks, looking up and cocking his head to the side. Another move he's perfected from living with Belle for so long.

"Because me and this book," I say, tapping on the cover. "Are going to go out there to talk Belle into getting some rain boots."

I already know it won't take any convincing for her to agree to this, but I don't want to tell him that.

The truth is, I just want the five minutes alone with her so I can show her the moment that nine year old Kayden made everything right again.

Chapter Nine

May 21, 2006

You know how people tell you that accidents happen and usually it's because you made some boneheaded mistake and they don't want you to feel bad about it?

I freaking love accidents!

Today was wicked. Like beyond epic, and it all started because my mom and Miss Grace made this tiny little mistake.

"Kayden, don't forget your jacket!" Mom said before we left and I didn't forget it, but I did forget to put my boots on.

That was the first mistake. The second one was when we stepped out the door, made it all the way across the street to meet Belle and her mom and we left the house without our umbrellas.

See? Moms can screw up too.

We got halfway to the park and the sky just exploded! Grace told my mom that God was having a laugh at our expense by throwing buckets of water down on us.

You know what I think? I think that just like the day at the park with Belle, he was trying to give us another great day.

Mom told me once that Belle doesn't really react well to temperature changes, so when it got cold and she stopped walking with me and went to her mom's side, it made sense. It's what happened when the rain started pouring down, making little rivers on the sidewalks that turned this mistake our moms made into the best thing ever.

She giggled. Like super loud, top of her lungs laughing!

So I laughed too and that's when it happened.

Belle whipped around super-fast, caught me, and in the time it took me to blink, ran close to me and jumped.

Splashing water all over my new pants, my jacket, and my shoes.

So I paid her back.

I jumped too!

We just kept jumping and laughing, and when I slipped and fell, she laughed even harder.

Her laugh is the **best thing ever**.

Way better than cars, cartoons on the weekend or playing basketball and hockey with Dean when he's not being a total asshead.

My mom yelled at us to stop screwing around, Grace did the same until she laughed and called us drowned rats, but we didn't care. We just kept jumping and having fun. We didn't stop until we made sure they were as wet as we were.

But the best part happened when the rain stopped.

She fell.

Okay so that's not the good part and I didn't laugh then, but what happened after was.

When I held out my hand for her to take, so I could help her up, she did it!

Belle doesn't like when I touch her. She moves away every time and it makes my stomach hurt when she does. It didn't happen this time though.

This time she took it and she didn't let go.

Even when my mom said it was time to go home a couple hours later, she didn't let go.

I didn't want her to.

Her hand was soft. Nice. Least it was until I started sweating like a pig.

Anyways, her doing that makes this the best day ever.

One I wanna remember forever, which is why I'm writing it here. Because I swear, when I'm bigger, I'm going to do it with her again.

Puddle jumping, hand holding, laughing.

All of it.

But there's something else I wanna do when I'm bigger.

With her skin all shiny from the raindrops, I'm going to pull her to me and kiss her.

I know that I said girls were gross and I'd never want to kiss them. They still are, and that's still true, but not Belle.

She's what my teacher Miss Smith called me when she asked Mr. Franks to help me with math.

Belle's the exception.

"Tristan read this?" she asks. "The whole thing?"

"Not sure how far he got into it, but yeah, he must have read pretty far if he knows about the puddle jumping."

"And you two talked through everything?"

"Not everything, but the fact that he talked to me at all, let alone opened up the way he did, is a step in the right direction. I mean, I feel like I might actually fix this when I was starting to think he would never forgive me."

"I told you he loved you, didn't I?" she says with a smirk. "It's fun when I'm right."

"Yes, baby. You were right. You're always right and I should know that by now." I concede with a laugh, more than happy to let her have her moment.

"Yes, you should." She grins, moving in until she's pressing her lips delicately against mine. "You should always listen to your know-it-all girlfriend."

"Fiancée." I softly correct her and with the proximity of her mouth to mine, I can feel the rise of her face as her smile grows.

"Everything." She counters as her fingers tap against the cover of the journal. The motion a gentle reminder of the last words I'd written.

"Yes, Belle. You've always been, and will always be, everything." I admit, nipping at her bottom lip with my teeth, bringing her to me, kissing her again, our tastes mingling and about to deepen it when a throat clearing slams the brakes on.

"I said you'd be doing this!" Tristan whines once we separate, and stomping across the room, shoves the movies he's chosen at me while Belle buries her face in my neck and laughs.

"It's her fault. If she wasn't so damn cute, I wouldn't need to kiss her every five seconds."

"Yeah, right." Tristan scoffs before moving across and throwing himself down on the sofa beside Belle. "Girls are gross."

"Tristan! They are not." Belle exclaims, turning to me and pouting.

Damnit. She knows exactly what buttons to push with me.

"She's got a point, man." I lean over and tell him. "But for the record, they were all gross to me too. Well, everyone but your sister." I add when Belle's elbow lifts and shoves against my side playfully.

"Yeah, I know. I read all about how much you loooove Belle."

With the way Tristan is rolling his eyes and fake gagging, I'm starting to see what Dillon meant by me being whipped.

"Alright, enough teasing Kayden. I think it's sweet." Belle says, turning her attention to the movies in my hand and then looking back to Tristan.

"Evil Dead? Really, Tris? Of all the movies we own, you want that one?"

"The bloodier the better." He grins.

"Two against one, baby." I say before reaching over and lifting my hand in the air. Tristan catching on and high fiving me before we both lean back and laugh at Belle as her eyes narrow and she pinches her nose and sighs.

"Fine, but when you're on the knees in the bathroom puking later because of all of the goo coming out of those people, I'm not helping."

Plucking her Kindle from the arm of the sofa, she stands, leaning over and kissing me softly before heading off down the hall to our room.

"Sorry for the cock-block." Tristan nudges me before turning his attention to the TV.

"I don't even wanna know where you learned that word."

"No, you don't."

"It was Dillon wasn't it?"

"I was sworn to secrecy."

Well, if I had any doubt who taught him what a cock block was, I don't anymore. Only Dillon would be stupid enough to swear someone to secrecy. Rolling my eyes with a grunt and taking the movies over to the DVD player, I slip the disc in and when I turn to head back to the sofa, making sure to take the long way around to grab the popcorn Belle made for us, he switches gears.

"So what did she say about puddle jumping?"

"Nothing. I never got the chance to ask her before you interrupted."

"If you spent more time talking and less time trying to stick your tongue down my sister's throat, she would have answered." He smirks.

"Shut it." I swat the back of his head. "I didn't get into it because I'm thinking it might mean more if she doesn't see it coming."

"You mean you wanna surprise her? Kayden..."

"I know she doesn't like surprises, but Tris, this one's different."

Pushing play on the DVD, I turn my attention to the movie as it starts, the opening credits scrolling by. After a few minutes, Tristan finally clears his throat and speaks. Letting me know when he does that he's been on the same page the entire time.

"It's supposed to rain tomorrow."

Then tomorrow it is.

It's time to make nine year old Kayden's wish come true.

I'm going to kiss her in the rain.

Chapter Ten

If someone had pulled me aside ten years ago and told me that one day in the future, I was going to be lucky enough to wake up with an angel, and better yet, that witnessing it every day after was going to be a bigger jolt to my system than a coffee in the morning, I would have laughed.

Back then, my biggest worry was what terror level color I was going to hit with Dean when he found out the shit I was causing.

It wasn't that I didn't want to be with someone, because deep down I think everyone wants that. It was more that I didn't believe it was something I deserved.

I guess when everyone that is supposed to give a shit about you walks out of your life and leaves you on your own with someone that on a good day can make the devil look like an angel, it's hard to see there being any other way things can go.

You accept that you're destined to be alone.

Only here I am, sharing not only a room and a bed with said angel, but I get the luxury of turning over in bed each morning and being met with the peaceful beauty of her face while she's still safe and secure in whatever hopeful dream she's currently dreaming.

Getting to use the few minutes before she senses my movement and wakes up, to really take her in. Things that when once we're up and moving and going about our day, I don't get to experience.

Like the way the stress lines in her face when she's buried in her course work is basically non-existent and her skin is evened out and feathery soft to the touch. Or feel the tickle that never fails to send a shiver through me when like every other day that's come before, I slip a fallen tendril of her hair through my fingers and slip it gingerly behind her ear.

My favorite part though, what really resonates and keeps me rooted firmly in place, the soft sigh that escapes when following the routine of the last year, I press my lips to her forehead, lingering for just a few second until the feel of her breath and her smile as it touches my skin pulls me away.

"Morning, Kay."

Brushing my nose against hers softly, I place my lips right on the tip and smile down at her.

"Morning, beautiful."

"You were doing it again, weren't you?"

Nothing gets by my girl. "Maaybe."

Reaching up and running a hand over the stubble on my face, she shifts up and nuzzles into it, sighing contentedly.

"I could get used to this look on you. You're becoming my very own teddy bear."

"Well, in that case," I softly chuckle. "I'm never shaving again."

"Mmmm, okay."

Shifting back on the bed, I tap the mattress a few times before reluctantly pulling away. If the plan Tristan and I put together last night is going to happen, we've got to get a move on.

With the weatherman actually getting it right for once and the rain pelting heavily into the roof above us, no doubt filling the streets with plenty of puddles for us to jump in, I don't want to waste a second.

"Rise and shine, baby. We've got places to be and people to conquer."

"We're taking over the world today, are we?" she asks, stretching out on the bed and groaning before sliding herself up and waking with a quick rub to her eyes.

"Same as every other day."

"Is Tristan up yet?"

"Not sure. I was about to go check."

"Can you turn the kettle on while you're out there?"

"Don't I always?"

Gifting me with one of the sweetest smiles, she nods and that's all it takes for me to turn back from the door, cross the room in the time it takes her to blink and lean down to where she rests against the headboard, bringing my hand to her face and pulling her lips to mine.

Sorry, God. You can't have her back. This angel is all mine.

Slapping me lightly when I finally break the kiss, she points to the door.

"Unless you want to spend the rest of this day in bed, go check on Tristan."

"Wait. You mean to tell me staying in bed all day with you is an option?" I tease.

"Not anymore. Time ran out."

"Fuck." I curse and when she giggles again, I press my luck and swoop in for another quick kiss.

"Go, Kayden."

"I'm going. I just needed another taste to keep me going until later."

Meeting the smirk on my face with one of her own, she points to the door again, all attempts at keeping a straight face failing when after a few seconds of attempted shooing, she cracks and laughs.

"Go make my tea or I'll withhold all future taste testing."

I've never left a room faster in my life.

*****

"How the hell are we going to get her out there?" Tristan whispers across the table once Belle has disappeared into the kitchen.

"I'm working on that."

"Yeah right." He calls me on my lie. "You're as stumped as I am. Maybe we should just tell her."

No way. If I tell her, she'll be expecting everything that happens. The kiss won't be a surprise. I know it's pretty much impossible to get anything past this girl, but this one thing, I really want to get over on her.

"I've got an idea, but it means getting help."

"What kind of help?"

"Your mom."

Realization dawns and just like that he's throwing his chair back from the table and racing back to the room. Forking up the last few bites of the remaining scrambled eggs on my plate up, I shove it in my mouth, swallowing it down quickly before pushing back from the table.

Taking my plate in and running it under the spray of the sink, I load it into the dishwasher and press my lips quickly to the top of her head.

"Where's Tris?"

"He thought he heard his phone so he went to get it."

As if he heard what I said or just read my mind, Tristan reappears and just like I hoped, does so with the phone outstretched toward his sister.

"Mom wants to talk to you."

Watching as Belle takes it and steps away from the running water, I turn off the tap and study her as she moves out from around the bar heading to the window and pulling the curtain back to peek outside.

Whatever Grace is saying playing perfectly into our plan as she sighs heavily into the phone before agreeing to run across.

"Shit." I curse and Tristan turns his attention away from Belle.

"What?"

"She's going to go for the umbrellas in the closet."

Grinning at me like he did the night before when he asked to watch a gory movie, it doesn't take me long to figure out that he's already taken care of the problem.

I've got to hand it to the kid. He's quick on his feet.

"They're under your old bed, but you didn't hear that from me."

Winking, he pulls away from his spot against the counter and heads over to where Belle is shoving her feet into her boots.

"What did she want?"

"Something came there for me and since it's a pretty thick envelope she wants me to run over and get it." She tells him before heading for the coat closet.

"Kay? Where's the umbrella?"

"It's not in there?" I play dumb and when her head comes out around the closet door and her eyes lock on mine, I almost cave. I'm not supposed to lie, even when it's like something as innocent as a kiss in the rain.

Shit.

"I think I took it with me the last time I was here." Tristan cuts in, saving my ass before I break. "Sorry, Belle."

"It's okay. That's why hoods were invented." She says, running her hands through his moppy hair. "I'll be right back."

The second she heads through the door and I hear it click behind her, I'm moving across the room and flipping the lock.

"Get your shoes on." I call to Tristan while I shove my own feet into my runners by the door.

Heading to the window and sneaking a peek through the curtain, I see her running up the lawn and hitting the steps to her mom's place. When Grace opens the door and it looks like they're talking, I turn back to Tristan.

"How are the puddles looking?"

"Like we'll be swimming for days."

"Perfect." He grins and that's when we do it. I flip the lock on the door and we head out, only instead of slipping my keys into the pocket of my jeans like always, I lock the door and book it quickly around the side of the house, tossing them to the ground.

I damn well know Belle isn't going to like me much when she realizes I've locked us all out of the house, but I'm hopeful that when she realizes why I'm doing it, she'll forgive me.

Even if she doesn't though, the kiss will be so damn worth the night sleeping outside I'll have in my future.

"Jeez!" Tristan yells when I make my way back over to where he's standing on the front lawn. "I forgot rain was this cold."

When I see he's not wearing a jacket, I immediately start seeing multiple nights of sleeping outside in my future. Belle is not only going to kill me for this, but so is Grace.

"Here," I shrug off my jacket and toss it at him. "Put that on."

"But—"

"But nothing." I cut him off. "My idea. My rules."

Slipping his arms through the jacket, he zips it up and turns just in time to see Belle racing back across the street towards us, her confused eyes filtering between us.

The coolness of the rain that's making quick work of soaking through my shirt, causing me to shiver and her to react by unzipping her own jacket and stretching it until it's acting as a partial shield.

"Kayden, what are you doing out here?"

"Seemed l-like a n-nice day for a swim." I joke and shaking her head at my nonsensical answer, she immediately slips her hands down into the front pocket of my jeans, searching for the one thing she's not going to find.

My keys are gone.

Let the games begin.

"Please tell me you didn't lock us out of the house." She pleads, and sensing Tristan's movement out of the corner of my eye, I shake my head and pull back, hoping as I do that I don't end up paying for what I know he's about to do.

Everything slows as he creeps up behind her as she continues to study me, attempting to figure out what the hell is going on, and at the exact moment he lifts off in order to hit the puddle directly behind where she's standing, she turns. The high velocity spray of the rain puddle doing what we wanted and completely drenching her.

"Holy!" she screams, the rest cut off as she jumps back from where Tristan stands hopping up and down laughing and closer to where I'm watching with amusement a few feet away. Her face changing when she locks her eyes on mine and finds the grin that even if I wanted to, I couldn't hide.

"You planned this." She states and with a quick nod, her eyes lower to the ground underneath her feet and when she looks back up, her blue eyes are calculated and she's smiling in a way that I haven't seen her before now.

Wickedly.

Oh boy. We're all gonna pay.

Bringing a hand to her lips in an effort to silence me to whatever it is she's planning on doing next, she spins around until she's locking eyes on Tristan, smirk gone and in its place, a look of sadness. One that once Tristan actually catches, has him pulling up beside her and wrapping his arms around her waist in an effort to make things right.

"I'm so sorry, Belle. I thought you would like it since you used to love going puddle jumping before." Tightening his grip around her waist, I hear him continuously apologize, and if I didn't know better, the act she's putting on would make me think he really had hurt her.

At least it would if she didn't turn back and smirk before distancing herself from him.

Pushing him just off to the side of the puddle of water that he'd just sprayed all over her and jumping down hard directly in the center of it a few seconds later, she sprays him. Water this time, not only soaking through her, but landing directly on target as the cool spray hits Tristan and ricochets back onto me.

My pants now matching what the downpour of rain had already done to my shirt, hitting and soaking all the way through, causing me to curse under my breath before jogging over to the puddle to her left and paying her back.

Over and over we chase each other around the front lawn, making sure to jump into any and all puddles of water we catch along the way. Until after stopping to pick Tristan up after taking one spot at a hard run, he'd slipped and landed straight into it and Belle fell to her butt right along with him.

The sound of both her laughter and his when after I come close enough to check on them and they yank me down, worth the level of sickness we're all going to end up getting once this is all over.

A sound that if I have my way, the rest of our lives will be filled with.

Seizing the opportunity when she turns to me and starts wiping away the stream of water from the rain that's now pouring down my face, I lean forward and right before I press my lips to hers, hear my second favorite sound escape from her lips.

The catch and release of her breath right before we connect.

Not even looking like we got into a fight with a storm and lost, our bodies and clothes so wet that we can actually hear the squishing taking place every single time we move, can take away from this moment.

The moment where I made one of my dreams come true by kissing the girl that *is* my dream.

Our lips dampened from the rain, soften them, making each touch and each probe once our lips part and our tongues meet, even more earth shattering than the last. With our hands in each other's hair, I pull her deeper into me, until her body is nestled into my lap, feeding on her even more, nipping at her lips and catching her tongue. Losing myself so completely in the moment that not even the faint sound of Tristan's groaning can break us apart.

This is so much more than a kiss.

This, right here on our front lawn, is happiness.

Freezing cold, soaked and generally sloppy happiness, but happiness all the same.

And Belle....well, she's the heart of it.

As the sound of Tristan's groaning about us being disgusting and needing to get a room gets louder, I pull back, but not away entirely. Choosing to do that only after I've kissed the top of her nose, her forehead and her hair and stood from the ground with my hand outstretched.

"What are you doing?" she eyeballs me before slipping her hand into mine.

"There's one other thing we have to do."

"You mean, there's more than just being drenched and kissed senseless on your agenda?"

"As a matter of fact," I say, pulling her to her feet and easily into my arms. "There is."

Slipping my hand into my pocket and grabbing my phone, I block it from the rain as I bring up another playlist I've got saved for the times I'm away and press play. The volume just loud enough to be heard around the sound of the sky opening up around us.

"Dance with me."

Chapter Eleven

"Kayden, put me down!" she squeals, wiggling her body in my arms as I carry her over the threshold of our room, making a beeline for the bed.

"You know," I tease. "I was planning on doing the gentlemanly thing here and helping you to the bed, getting you out of those wet clothes and into a warm bubble bath. But with you wiggling around like that, I'm pretty sure I lost all ability to be a gentleman."

Belle, from the moment I met her was never like other girls, and it wasn't anything to do with her diagnosis. She was different because for some reason that years ago, I don't think I was able to explain, I just knew she deserved better.

That's not to say there haven't been moments over the last few years where I haven't wanted to just throw her down and have my way, preferably on any surface that we may have nearby. Because I have.

A lot.

But just like that night on the beach where I wanted her first time to mean something, mean everything really, I do every other time too. So the need to take things slow, cherish the person I'm lucky enough to have in my arms, wins out.

Even in a moment like right now, where the need to just rip the clothes from her body with the way she keeps brushing herself against my dick, is screaming to win out.

That isn't what this is about, though.

Being out there on our front lawn while her brother found every imaginable way to soak her, laughing and carrying on like we were nine years old again; that was the memory I wanted.

Seeing her in the aftermath, though, is *definitely* a bonus.

She's probably looked this way more than once over the years, but there's something in the way she is now that's making me actually shut up and take notice of it.

Depositing her down onto the bed, I place a kiss to her forehead before attempting to go to work. The flushed cheeks, wide dancing eyes, and crooked smile all there to greet me when I pull away, only making the need for what I want to happen now even more important.

"Lie back."

Doing as I ask, she rests her body back onto the blanket, shifting herself further back onto the bed and away from the edge. The hooded look in her eyes pausing me in my task as I take in her positioning and the words that fall from her lips next.

"What if I said I didn't want you to be a gentleman, Kay? What would you do then?"

Down, Walker.

I know what she's doing, I even know why, but I can't let that take over here. My girl deserves better than that. I want her, no question, and she's going to know just how much soon enough, but not if I let the urge override the feeling.

I'm not seventeen and horny anymore, and she's not some random girl that if I could just get past the shit in my head, could relieve me of it.

She's Belle.

My Belle.

"I would do this." I say, straddling my body over hers and leaning in to kiss her lips, surrendering to the feel of them against mine for a moment before pulling away. "And then go back to doing what I should be doing."

"Which is?" she asks, her words breathless, filled with a need that while I've gotten used to hearing, still manages to take my breath away every single time it happens.

One almost as potent as mine for her.

Almost.

"Getting you out of these wet clothes."

Shifting over to her side, my hands lower to the button on her jeans, popping it out and pausing whatever it was she planned to say next, filling the space instead with the sound of her light gasp before she shimmies her legs and moans.

What she knows will be my undoing.

Lowering the zipper, I lift her up off the bed and begin the slow process of sliding her jeans, which feel as though they're permanently attached to her body, down. Slipping them around her ankles until one slight kick from her feet has them landing on the floor with a heavy thump.

A sound she obviously seems to find amusing as she begins to laugh softly before I move back up and silence her with another kiss.

A kiss that before it can deepen, Belle is the one pulling back from. Lifting up off the bed just enough, she lets me know with just a look why she pulled away as her arm lifts into the air and she's attempting to take her shirt off. Making sure that as she pulls it off that it makes it way to the floor, before wrapping her arms around my neck pulling me down to the bed with her and kissing me again.

This time, her tongue quickly probing my lips, tasting them before making its way inside and tangling itself up in my ready and willing one. The vibration of her moan mixing with the rawness of mine as we hungrily taste each other, and as my hands begin to slide down her body, feel each other.

Dampness from the rain drenching through her clothes making her body slick to the touch, but warmer than I expect, only serving to make me hungry for more.

Pulling away and nibbling softly when she groans from the separation, I begin kissing down her neck. Pausing when I get to her shoulder and am able to bear witness to the droplets of water that despite being covered, still managed to pool there and are now making her skin glisten.

This is even better than I imagined.

Laying here with me, exposed but for the bra and panties I still have yet to remove, she's the most beautiful thing I've ever seen. Her skin literally glowing from the effect of the rain and the kiss we just shared.

I'm seeing Belle for the first time.

Bare and exposed. Beautiful and willing. Soft, needy and all mine for the taking.

Pressing my lips to a droplet of water before it has a chance to cascade down her shoulder and be lost forever, I taste it before continuing down. Succumbing to the feel of her as my touch, my embrace, and the kisses I rain down on her cause her to arch into me.

Her next words, short, breathless, filled with want and need, but still uniquely Belle.

"You're being a little unfair, don't you think?"

"Hmmm? How so?" I murmur before snagging her lip with my teeth and pulling her into yet another passionate kiss. "I think this is very fair. I can lay you back and kiss away every drop of rain from your body."

Shifting upward, she takes me off guard as she pushes into me, laying me out flat on my back as she takes control of the moment and straddles me, the only giveaway of what's to come present in the flame of desire I now see blazing in her eyes.

A fire that's only for me.

"It's not fair because I can't do the same to you. I can't feel the warmth of your skin against mine or the wetness from you mixing with mine." She smiles down before her hands lower to my own pants and she rubs ever so softly over my own arousal. My aching and now almost painful need to have her.

"I think it's only fair we even the odds."

Oh God.

She can even whatever she wants. Hell, with the way she's brushing her hand harder over my erection now, she can take the lead. Win this game of ours. Hell, she already has won.

Belle always wins.

Grabbing a hold of my hand, she pulls me up and steadying myself on the mattress, I attempt to contain myself when her fingers brush against my stomach as she lifts the water logged shirt up and over my head. Where it lands, where it even goes once it's peeled from me, I don't know because my attention, it focuses downward as just like I'd done, she makes quick work of the buttons keeping me contained.

Freeing me of the restraints, but halting her before she can continue the same movement with my boxers, my hand finds her cheek, cupping it tightly and I bring her lips crashing down to mine again. The rope that up until now had been restraining me in the way I needed it to snapping, until all we are is a mash of lips touching, bodies rubbing and hands feeling.

Her moans matching the veracity of my own until the room is drenched in the sounds of them. My name falling softly from her mouth when I break away for air and hers catching and releasing roughly when after needling my skin with her hands, she again slips down and begins removing the layer that stands between us.

Answering her need with my own, I begin rubbing my fingers on the outline of her panties, over her warmth and what I just know is her readiness for what is about to happen next. What I'm rewarded with when after she arches, the hot breath of her moan in my ear pushing me forward, I slip my fingers inside, teasing her.

"Kayden..." My name like a reverent prayer as it falls hungrily from her lips.

"You. Are. So. Beautiful." I tell her between kisses, as I hook my fingers into her panties and begin to slide them down. Continuing to move one finger and then two from my other hand inside her, struggling to remain in control when she writhes against me the deeper I let myself go.

My lips on a path of their own as they find every drop of wetness that glistens and makes her skin shine, from her lips, to her shoulder, down her chest and over her stomach, and all the way up her arms until my teeth are again grazing the tight skin of her neck.

My fingers slipping from inside when her body stills and her soft needy voice pleads with me for more.

"Now, Kay."

"Now what, baby?" I ask, needing to hear the words that will match the intoxicating look I'm now seeing in her eyes.

"I need you...now. Make love to me, please."

Unhooking her bra and shedding the remainder of our clothes, bringing down the last remaining barrier that stands between the two of us coming together, that's exactly what I do.

I love her.

Chapter Twelve

"Mom?" I call out, rubbing my eyes and moving across the hall.

Through the crack in the doorway, where she left it ajar, I can see her moving frantically back and forth between the dresser and the bed. Bundles of clothes in her hand. So much of it that pieces of it are falling to the floor, but her frantic movements and attention to the task blinding her to it.

Slapping my hand on the door with another quick jab at my eyes, clearing the sleep from them, I push it back and step in. The low squeal of the hinges pulling her from what she's doing and focusing her attention on the intrusion.

Whatever she's expecting to see causing her entire body to freeze in place and jump back, her hand flying to her chest and clutching until she finally takes a breath when she sees it's me.

"What's going on?"

Taking in what I couldn't see before, I catch sight of the suitcase first and the colorful assortment of clothes practically pouring out of it. Looking over to the dresser, I see that's she made it through four of the six and has the fifth one already open and ready to clean out.

"Are we going somewhere?"

Stepping toward me, her movements slow, each step deliberately placed on certain parts of the carpeted floor, she pulls me straight into the warmest and tightest embrace.

"Yeah, Kay-Kay, we are."

The tremble in her voice should alert me to the fact that wherever we're going isn't going to be a good thing, but my need for her smile wins out.

I can't help it. I smile. Get excited. We're finally going to get away from here.

"Should I go pack too?"

"Yes, baby. Make sure your brother is up and get him to put a bag together too. We don't have much time."

Her final words are all the motivation I need as I pull away and speed back out across the hall. Diving onto the bed, I shake Dean awake, flinching the second his body moves, knowing what's coming when reality sets in and he figures out it's me jumping all over him.

Backing up and heading to the closet, I pull the duffel my mom bought me a couple of months ago down off the top shelf just in time to hear Dean growling from across the room.

"What the fuck?"

"Mom said get your ass up and pack a bag. We're leaving." I tell him as I shoot around to the dresser and begin pulling clothes out the same way I'd seen her do, shoving them all in the bag. Not stopping, even when he curses the same question at me again until I've gotten everything I think I need and the bag is zipped shut.

"Come on, Dean. Mom said we don't have a lot of time."

His eyes cloud over before his lips drop downward into a scowl. Having been on the receiving end of that look more than once over the last few months, I know it's not good. I want to question if this is about the way I woke him up or something else, but before I have the chance to, he's barrelling past me, his shoulder shoving hard into mine as he stalks out of the room and across the hall.

Voices raise and just as I'm about to head over and make them stop, I hear a crash and Dean is back in our room, following my earlier movements and yanking a bag down angrily before proceeding to fill it. Cursing under his breath and complaining the entire time.

"What the fuck are you smiling at?" he yells when he pulls the zipper across the bag and looks up, catching me staring.

"Nothing."

"Bullshit. You think this is a good thing don't you?"

Of course I do, and deep down I know he does too. He told me so. One night when he wasn't being a total ass, he told me how he feels about Mom and Dad fighting. He also said he didn't think it would ever end. Even with him out of the house, it seemed he was *always going to end up coming back here and laying into the woman he calls his wife. The supposed love of his life.*

Is love really supposed to be this violent?

I have half a mind to ask Dean about it now, but with the look of death he's giving me, I somehow doubt he'd give me the answer I'm after. Besides, I've seen the way real love works.

All I have to do is go to Belle's house and it's there. It fills the place.

Pretty sure love oozes off the walls there.

I want to go there.

Realizing that Belle Reagan is who I consider my happy place has another stupid grin forming on my face and it doesn't take long after Dean catches it for him to be across the room and hovering over me, his fist shoving into my stomach, wiping it away completely.

Go ahead. Take the smile off my face all you want. You won't take it out of my head. I'll never let you do that.

It's a silent threat, but one I repeat over and over until my mom interrupts us, taking in our positions before telling us to knock it off because we have to go.

Slinging the bag over my shoulders and feeling the weight dragging me down almost instantly, I move as quickly as I can, following her out. A grumbling under his breath Dean right behind me. The heat of his breath practically searing a hole into my skin from its warmth.

It's only when we get outside and she starts making a break for it across the street, after a quick warning hush that I realize what's going on. What she's doing.

Running as fast as my small as shit legs can go, I catch up to her, grabbing her elbow with my hands and getting her to slow down.

"I thought we were leaving?"

"We are. I just have to make a quick stop here first." She tells me before making quick work of the grass that leads to Belle's front door. With Dean pulling up the rear, we make it up to the front step and instead of ringing the doorbell or knocking like we have every other time, she twists the door handle and steps

straight in. Ushering us in quickly and peeking her head out the door and looking around once we're in before turning back to us and shutting it.

Hearing the click of shoes on the stairs, I turn toward the sound, but it's not the person now rushing them that I take in when I do. It's her.

At the top of the stairs, she sits quietly. Eyes widened and focused straight on me before flicking over to my brother and back again.

Taking a step, ready to climb the stairs to her, especially after what I thought about earlier, Grace's hand landing on my shoulder halts me.

"Not right now, Kayden."

Why the hell not? She's my best friend. I wanna go upstairs and be with her.

Feeling her eyes on me, I look to Belle again and that's when I see it. Her eyes are filled with water. Tears. The front of her nightgown stained and her lip is pouting. Maybe even quivering.

It makes sense now.

She's had one of her bad days. She's extra scared today and when she gets like that, Grace says I need to give her time. The problem is, I don't want to give her time.

She needs me, same as I need her.

Parting my lips, I mouth silently to her and that's when I see it.

The exact reason Belle is my happy place.

Her lip pulls in and quirks up in the tiniest smile at my words, making what I just thought true.

We need each other.

I don't know what's going on with my mom right now, why there's such a rush to leave or why we had to stuff our duffel bags with clothes, but right here in this moment, I don't give a shit.

I'm where I wanna be.

Right where I belong.

"Soon."

Awakening from my haze at the feel of my body being shaken, my eyes pop open and they're met with the sky blue warmth I'd just been so lost in.

"There you are." She says, wrapping her arms around me and squeezing me tight before shifting and curling herself around my now suddenly wide awake body.

"What happened?"

"You were dreaming. Calling out to me, actually. Repeating the same word over and over. I'm not sure how long you were doing it, but when I finally woke up and heard you, I tried everything to get you to wake up."

The dream. The reason I'm laying here in bed with the blankets kicked completely off, sweat seeping from every pore, and why her eyes look so damn worried staring back at me.

That wasn't a dream for fuck sakes. That was the beginning of a nightmare, and one that despite the fact that I am going to tell her what it was about, I'd rather not dive back into.

Yesterday was so perfect. Kissing her in the rain, Tristan snickering behind us when I finally did it and then drenching us in water. Then after bringing him home, taking her back to the house and standing in the middle of our room, watching her as the rain made her skin glisten the same damn way it did when we were nine and I was overtaken by a need to experience her like this.

Love her after the rain touched her.

Lost myself in her.

Telling her what I was dreaming about will take the beauty of yesterday and twist it, the same way I did the night we talked about Sammy and everything else came spilling out.

"I was dreaming about the day my mom left." I blurt, and she reacts by burrowing herself even deeper into my arms.

"Soon." She whispers, and her earlier words about me repeating that word come back.

"It's what I mouthed to you when my mom first brought us over. Your mom wouldn't let me go to you, and seeing you crying at the top of the stairs made me sick. So I did the only thing I could."

"You told me soon because you wanted me to know you'd get to me."

"Yeah." I admit and that's when her lips find my chest and she's brushing them gently over where my heart rests. The part that she owns.

"You held my hand that day. You never let it go and back then, after she took off and Dean told me she was gone, I held it against you. I thought you were holding my hand so tight because you knew she left me. I hated you for it. When you held my hand it was supposed to mean good things. Not the worst thing."

"I never knew, Kayden. All I was sure of was that I wanted to hold your hand."

Shifting in the bed, I take her chin in my hand and lift it up to where our eyes can meet and running a finger over her lips, I lean in and kiss her, while at the same time, slipping my hand down and finding hers. Locking our fingers together the way she did then.

And just like then, she gives me everything I need the second we're joined. Reminding me not of my mother leaving and the impact the event had on me all those years ago, but of the realization that nine year old me had before it even happened.

She's my happy place.

"Promise me something?" I ask, my lips so close to her skin I swear I can actually see the words forming on the peach of her flesh.

"Anything."

"Whatever you read next. Whatever we read in the journal from back then, promise me you'll never let go." Slipping my hand out of hers, but not pulling away, I lift it in the air between us and place them together palms facing each other. "Take my hand and promise that you'll never let it go again."

Lowering her fingers down into the spaces in mine, the ones that I swear with the way they perfectly align, were made for her and her alone, she gives me her answer in the only way she can.

Tightening the lock our fingers have to one another, she nods slowly as she brings her lips to mine. Her action less about a kiss and more about fulfilling my need for skin to skin connection.

And just like I heard her love for me loud and clear three years ago, I hear it again now.

Straight in my heart.

Chapter Thirteen

November 10, 2006

Something's not right.

We've been at the Reagan's most of the day. Mom's been gone for hours, it's nighttime now and even though she swore she'd be back for us, we're still here.

I keep asking Grace when my mom is coming back, but she doesn't say anything. She just sniffles and turns away.

Maybe she's just getting sick or something.

I just wish someone would tell me where Mom is. Why she left earlier and hasn't called to check in or come back and got us the way she promised before she hugged me and walked out the door.

Or at least explain why Dean won't stop staring out the window across the street at our house.

He was there when Grace finally let me go to Belle and there when I came downstairs with her a few hours later. He stood there while we all had dinner and he's still there now.

A few times when she leaves the room to go check on him, I can hear them talking and I swear once I even heard sniffling coming from him too. Since he never gets sick, even when I wish he would so I wouldn't have to deal with him, I know it's gotta be something else causing it.

Something is wrong.

My mom is gone and I'm here surrounded by people that aren't her.

I'm alone.

The first time I got up the nerve to ask Dean, he grunted at me and then went back to looking out the window. And the last? He grunted and swore at me under his breath before stomping off to the kitchen. I heard slamming of cupboards and then the shake of the fridge and then he was there again, drink in hand, at the window.

Why won't anyone tell me anything?

I asked Belle and she cried. A lot. I couldn't calm her down. She was rocking back and forth and I had to put my hands up to block her head from hitting my chest. She hits really hard when she's like that.

I don't even know why she's doing it. We were fine for a long time. I even got her to smile, kind of. I like when she smiles, but just like mom is gone it seems like her smiles are too.

When Belle cries, my stomach hurts and all I want to do is cry too, so when she did it and wouldn't stop, I lowered my hands away, let her bang against me even though it stung and I cried too.

If anyone wonders what happened, I'll just say Belle hurt me since crying is for pussies according to Dean. But it wasn't Belle.

I can take what she gives me, especially if it helps her.

What I can't take is not knowing.

How lost I feel.

How alone.

My brother is here and I still feel like I'm in a room full of aliens or something. I've been abducted and no one speaks my language.

Mom...where the hell are you? When can we go home? I like Belle's bed, but I miss mine. I miss you reading me a story. I miss our jokes when no one else is around to hear. I know what you said about me and Dean, but I don't believe you meant it. You were just so sad. It's just sad words.

Please just come home so we can forget you even said them.

I miss you.

It's happening again. Freaking waterworks. I know what Dean said about them and how guys just aren't supposed to let it happen. I also remember the threat that if he saw me doing it, he'd beat them out of me. Right now I don't care about any of that because it feels okay.

It makes the pain stop.

I don't have to rub my skin until it bleeds to try and stop the ache that's there when I cry. It just settles itself.

Please, Mom. Come back.
I wanna go home.

"Belle..." I plead quietly, closing my eyes tight and rubbing the ache in the center of my chest. "I—I can't."

Feeling the weight lift from the center of my lap, I follow her as she moves the book away completely, laying it to rest on the opposite side before resting her head against mine.

There's not a lot here about my mom. I know this. I also know why that is.

It's because I didn't believe it.

Couldn't believe it at first.

Then, when it sunk in, I couldn't confront it. I couldn't admit that she walked out on us without so much as a glance back to make sure we were okay. I couldn't deal with the fact that all of the shit she'd told me over the years was actually true and we'd let her down.

We were so bad she couldn't stand to be our mother anymore.

I couldn't deal with any of it, and with the way I just want to rub my skin raw in an attempt to rid myself of that same fucking ache I felt then, before Grace and Dean even sat me down and told me what was really going on, I still can't.

"Thank you." I somehow manage to choke out after sitting in what feels like silence for hours but couldn't have been more than a minute or two. My mind flooded with every single thing I thought and felt from that day and the first few after it as reality had the chance to settle in.

Or with what happened the day Grace let us head back home, had beat into me.

"Why are you thanking me?"

"I know you didn't have any control over the way you were reacting the day she left. That it had nothing to do with her leaving or Dean being there, but baby, you crying and wanting to hit something...hit me, it helped."

I don't even have to meet her eyes to know she won't believe me. Seeing her meltdowns as something bad and not the saving grace they were that day. I guess, when you live with them as long as Belle has, it isn't a good thing, but for me, that day especially, it definitely was.

She opened the door and let me feel without consequence.

"You're welcome." She says with a gentle squeeze, burying her face into my shoulder and breathing in and out evenly. "The truth is, I just thought I made things worse."

"Never. Even when I was being a complete prick, it wasn't your fault. None of it was. Even if at the time I really wished it could have been."

For a while after my mom took off, things stayed pretty much the same way as they were before. I was over at their house as much as possible when I wasn't being forced to go to school every day. I still looked forward to being there and hated leaving at night in order to go home to Dean and his ranting.

His excessive drinking and nights full of hatred and loathing.

The blame being tossed at Belle's feet happened a year later.

"Kayden, can I ask you something?"

"Anything."

"I know you probably don't want to get into it, but a couple of days after Mom sent you home, you came back over after school with a bunch of cuts on your face. Mom used to tell me that you were fighting at school, acting out because you were trying to deal with your mom leaving, but I didn't believe her. I still don't."

She didn't believe it because she knew me better than anyone.

Sure, I became really aggressive after she split, but after all the crap at home, I'd learned how to fight and it wasn't often I had marks to show for it.

Unless the marks *came* from home.

"It was Dean. It was always him, Belle."

"How bad was it?" she murmurs softly, her attempt to not push me evident, but unnecessary given the road I'm already on.

"No worse than the stuff that was going on before."

"Was it like the day I found you on the floor?"

My head starts moving of its own volition. Nothing was quite as bad as what Belle walked in on senior year.

That was the end result, not the beginning.

"The first night we went home, things seemed okay. I was in my room alone, Dean was out in the living room drinking. With him, that was pretty standard though. It only turned nasty after he started inviting people over. He wanted to put on a show at that point and ended up using me to do it."

"How?"

"Called me out of the room saying he wanted to run through drills with me. Combat techniques. He wanted to be sure that I didn't turn into a pussy like our mother."

"Kay..."

"I know, Belle. But if I don't get it out now, I never will. You knew the gist of what was going on here. What you could see after the fact anyway. Maybe it's time I dealt with what got me there."

"Okay..." she answers, the word trepid and unsure. The way they should be. No one should ever have to deal with this kind of nightmare. Least of all her.

"I blocked the first few attempts. He couldn't get a hit off and when he attempted to take me off my feet, that wasn't working either. But considering how easily he'd been able to do it before, I knew it was booze causing his delay. I just didn't expect the adrenaline rush I ended up having the more we went at it. How into it I got. Soon we were sparring, and even though they weren't all that hard, I got a few good hits in. Made his drunk ass stumble. But I got cocky showing off for his buddies, and when I turned my attention away it all changed."

"Changed how?"

It's weird how things that happened years before, ones that you haven't even really thought about in forever, are always just there. They never really go away. They only seem to gain more color and vibrancy when you're forced to remember them.

"He didn't hold back. He was pissed drunk, but vile. I think that was the night I finally learned the truth."

"What truth?"

"How he really felt about me."

✳✳✳✳✳

Rubbing at my jaw, now stinging from the impact of Dean's fist as it sideswiped my face, I steel myself for what comes next and ready my body for his next move.

"Come on, pretty boy. Stop tearing up and show me what you got!"

I'll show him tearing up when I take his head clear off.

Lunging at him, I realize two seconds too late that he's moved from his position and come crashing down to the floor hard as my sock hooks onto the ridge in the carpet. Swallowing down the anger at the wails now filling the room from Dean and his idiotic friends, I attempt to get back to my feet.

I'm just not quick enough.

Struggling against Dean's meat filled arm as it comes across my neck and he pulls back tight, our bodies so close I can actually feel the movement of his breath between our clothes, I shift my arm in an attempt to elbow him off me.

A mistake he catches when with his free hand he halts me, leaning in as close as he possibly can, his beer mixed with rum breath running hot against the side of my face. The smell enough to make me want to concede defeat by passing out. Out of breath but still managing to find the words, he says things that despite seeing it in actions over the last few years, he's never actually outright admitted to.

"It's your fault she's gone, you know. She told me just how pathetic she thought you were. How your incessant need to be close to her was driving her fucking crazy. She never wanted you in the first place. None of us did. God. Dad was so fucking pissed when he found out she was knocked up. He knows you're not his. That you're just a dirty bastard not even a mother could love."

Doubling over when after shoving me down the floor he lands a hard knee down into my back, I bring my hands up over my face, before resting them over my ears, having heard more than enough and needing to block out whatever shit he's going to spew next.

What turns out to be a fail as he wastes no time yanking my hands away and continuing his verbal assault. What hurts even more than the random hits he gets off, and what I would gladly give myself over to physical torture in order to stop.

"I hate that she left me here with you. That I've got to get up every fucking day and actually take care of your blubbering, worthless ass. You're pathetic, Kayden. The worst kind of brother. No one wants you. Not me, not Dad and as you can see..." he laughs sadistically, pulling back just enough to enjoy the laugh with his friends. "Not Mom."

"You're lying!" I yell, waiting until he's down close enough again and using every bit of strength I have to turn myself just enough to get a shot off. A shot that once it connects with his face, I'm sure has broken my hand.

Breathe Kayden. Close your eyes, keep breathing and you'll be out of here soon enough. Back across the street where it's safe.

Where you're loved.

As Dean begins another assault, retaliation for the mark I'm sure I've left on his face, I let go. Close my eyes and begin to succumb to the black that his ugly ass school ring drenches me in the more he attacks.

"Walker boys aren't bad. Just you are." He hisses through his teeth as spots begin to form in front of my eyes and the faint scent of blood as it breaks through my now open skin begins to fill the air.

"And if that selfish bitch ever comes back, I'm going to show her just how bad."

☆☆☆☆☆

"It's okay, Kay. You're not with Dean anymore. You're with me and you're safe." I hear her soothing as I come out of the memory. Wetness evident as it coats my face, but her wrapped so completely in me that her hair has taken the majority of it. Soaked them up.

Erased them.

"I did it." I breathe out, the ramifications of Dean's final words crackling in the air around me.

"Did what?"

"I thought I was fighting back. I thought I was fighting *against* him, but that wasn't what happened at all. I let him beat me. I let him change me. I let it all happen and didn't do a damn thing to stop it."

As her hold on me grows tighter, I ready myself for the argument that's bound to come. What I'm damn sure she's not going to believe because even though she has no issue calling me on my crap, she's not going to share the same belief that this was all my fault.

"I gave up."

"You were nine." She states, right on cue and I shake myself so strongly in denial that her hold falls away until it's just me.

Exactly the way it was then.

Always just me.

"I was nine, not two. I knew right from wrong, good from bad, love from hate. I knew it all!"

"And he was your brother. You loved him. You gave up because you loved him."

"No! Belle, don't you get it? I gave up and became the monster because it was fucking easier. What I didn't wasn't noble, so stop trying to make it seem like it was."

The position of the cushion she's been sitting on changes, and I know I've gone too far. Lost myself so deep into past bullshit that I've turned back into the very thing I've spent three years trying to escape.

I'm putting it on her.

Making her the bad guy.

The same way I did then.

"Belle..."

"No, Kayden." She halts me. "You're right. You did take the easy way out. You made the choice to do the things you did to me and others. I'm not going to excuse any of that, but back then, after your mom left and the things your brother did...they aren't all on you. What I said is still right. You went through all of that because you wanted something different. Thought if you just hung in there, it could and would be better."

"I should have, I don't know, fought harder. Taken him out before he could make good on his promise to ruin me."

"Kay..."

"I could have done it, Belle. I wanted to do it so badly. I wanted to end him. End it. I could have done it, but he was right. I was too weak." Pausing as a realization hits me straight between the eyes, I laugh and as expected, she looks at me like I've lost my mind.

"What's so funny?"

"All those years we spent together and I never saw it. It was staring me in the face the entire time and it took years for it to finally sink in."

"What are you talking about?"

"You, Belle. If I had just stayed with you instead of going off the rails the way I did, I would have been able to do it."

"Do what?" she presses, her eyes curving in and becoming increasingly more confused.

"Beat him. Be better. Stronger."

"Kayden," she sighs. "I don't understand what you're trying to say."

"You were the strong one. *You.* Every day, you woke up and did what you had to do even though I know you didn't understand any of what was going on with you or why. You wore the same face, even when things may have been falling apart. You never lost heart or hope. You never showed weakness. And before you argue and tell me that you did, I'm gonna stop you because I'm not talking about your accidents, the meltdowns or any of the other things you did back then that to everyone else looked like you were breaking down. I'm talking about the way that you got up again after one of those episodes and kept going. You never gave up."

I realized very quickly after our reconnection that she was the stronger of the two of us, but after everything we've brought to light over the last few days, it's never been clearer. Belle went through hell and she never let it break her.

She's stronger than she thinks she is.

Belle is stronger than all of us.

"If I'd clued in sooner to it, I could have used your strength. Stopped all of this before it ever got to the point that it did. I could have been the person you needed me to be."

"I only ever needed you to be you, Kayden. Whatever or whoever that was. As long as it was you, then I had everything I needed. Lover, fighter, bully or the bullied. I only ever wanted you."

"So you would have been okay with the person I became?"

"No," she admits. "I don't think anyone wanted that, but the boy that kept hoping for a better outcome, never stopped wanting that end, yes. I wanted him because he was you. Then and now. Do you wanna know what I thought about after I made sure you were alright the night of homecoming?"

She could want to recite a fast food menu from one of the drawers in the kitchen and I'd want to hear it, so her question is silly. Of course I want to know. Every single thought she has is important. Especially with the way everything went down that night and what happened after.

"I was so happy I got to you in time." She admits once I've given her the go ahead with a slight nod. "But not because I was there to protect you physically, and not even because it was the first time I spoke so openly."

"Then why?"

"Because despite the humiliation I went through at your hand, the pain of losing you years before, and the sting of that loss that I lived with every day until the day you drove me home that first time, I prevented Dean from stealing the rest of you."

"What do you mean?"

"The night you kissed me for the first time, I saw it. The look in your eye. I saw the real you. No matter how hard you tried to distance yourself from it, it was still there, Kayden. Coming into the house that night and seeing you on the floor, broken, bruised, but still breathing, I knew what I had to do. I had to stop Dean from robbing you of it. Of yourself."

"You saved me."

"No, Kay. I might have been there and stopped things, but I didn't do the saving. You did."

It's on the tip of my tongue to argue, but with the determination in her eyes, the rightness I can see there, the truth that she wears so strongly it radiates from her eyes, I can't do it.

I can't take away her belief.

I won't.

Not when I'm pretty sure even with my own argument, she's right.

"I knew I had to protect the look I saw that night, Kayden. Even if we hadn't become what we are and we'd gone back to the way things were, as long as that stayed, things would be fine. You were still in there and you'd be okay."

Belle has always been a deeper thinker than the rest of us and here's proof.

She saw something in me then that for whatever reason, I couldn't or didn't want to see. Something I'm sure she's been seeing all along.

Me.

The me I was when I was with her.

The person I always want to be.

"Thank you." I murmur, reaching across until my hand is wrapping securely around hers and pulling her close to me again.

"Thank you for seeing what I couldn't."

"Always." She smiles, patting my leg before sliding off the sofa and hopping to her feet. "Now, come on. We've got some breakfast to make and actually eat this time."

Taking her outstretched hand in mine and letting her pull me to my feet, I wrap my arms around her and we walk to the kitchen. As she steps away from me, busying herself at the fridge, grabbing ingredients for whatever she's got in mind to eat, I watch her. All the while swallowing the lump beginning to grow despite the calm way we seemed to end the latest walk down memory lane.

A lump I know with everything coming up next in our journaling journey, is a precursor to the storm that's brewing.

I just hope when it's all said and done, this time, I can get us both out unscathed.

Chapter Fourteen

January 4, 2008

Everyone leaves.
It's all lies.
Everyone is full of crap.
It's like Dean says. Everyone is full of shit. We're all just swimming in bullshit.
I just never thought she'd be a part of it.
Not her.
Not my Belle.
But it's true. She's just like everyone else.
She's bad. A liar.
Why else would she cry when she caught me doing it and then call me the same name my mom did?
Why would she look so pathetically sad if she wasn't a part of this?
If she didn't know all this time that my mom was planning on leaving without me.
All this time I thought Belle was my friend, but she wasn't. She's just like everyone else. All sweet to your fucking face and then the worst kind of mean behind your back.
Her and that stupid mom of hers. The one I liked calling Auntie Grace.
I never want to see them again.
I hate them.
Want to hurt them the same way they did me.
I heard Grace talking. I heard the whispers and what she said to Belle before I told her to go to screw herself and left the house.

They've both known about my mom all this time. Known about what happens to me across the street and want it to keep happening.

She makes me sick.

I hate her.

I love her.

I miss her.

I want to hurt her.

Why Belle? Huh? Why did you have to be like everyone else? Why couldn't you just tell me that my mom was leaving and I was gonna get stuck with Dean?

I could have run away. Begged your mom to keep me forever so we'd never have to be apart. I could have helped her and earned my place. Anything but this.

Anything but the lies and secrets.

I thought we felt the same. I thought I meant everything. The same way you mean everything to me.

Why did you lie? Why do you hate me so much? Why do you have to make my chest hurt? Why does it have to hurt so bad that I can't breathe?

I want to hit something. Force my fingers in as tight as they can go and just unload on something. A person, a face, a wall. Something. Anything that will make this pain go away.

I miss my mom.

I want her to come home. Show her that Walker boys can be good enough. That we can be awesome. I want her to see that I'm not him, and if she promises to stay, things will get better.

I'll make them better.

But as much as I miss her and can feel my chest caving in on itself...the pain isn't all for her.

It's Belle.

If getting the hell away from her and her lies is the right thing, why does it feel like something is missing?

Oh right. It's because that stupid girl across the street ripped my heart out and kept it.

Belle has my heart.

Good.

I didn't need that piece of shit anyway.
My heart or her.
I'm better off alone.

"I always wondered..." she whispers as she closes the book and taps on the cover. "I spent a lot of time trying to figure out when everything changed. How one day we were fine. You were still coming over and playing with me just like always and then suddenly you were spitting on me whenever you got close enough to actually make contact and cursing me under your breath whenever we passed on the street. I guess I know now."

How do I explain this so she'll understand more than just the ten year old ramblings in the book? How do I tell the woman I love that all it took was a name, a look, and a conversation she had with her mom that she probably doesn't even remember, for me to turn my back on her?

I can't. There's no way it will make sense. I'm not even sure it makes sense to me anymore.

I was ten. I was already angry, but considering the combative relationship I had with Dean at the time, especially since he had his own issues with Mom leaving and being left alone with me, it had reached an all-time high. The only time I can even remember being happy before I blew everything to shit being those days with her.

Those few hours where like she said, it was like nothing had changed and it was us against the world.

Belle, until that day when she hugged me, rubbing her hands on my back and called me Kay-Kay like my mom, was the only one I wasn't mad at.

Until I was.

"Grace told you she was sorry, Belle. Sorry she didn't do more to stop what was happening to me. You nodded. All you did was nod your head and for me, it was like you were admitting to knowing things. The same way she did. I blamed you for taking my mom away and not keeping her here. I blamed you for everything."

Even after we got together in high school, I never told her the reason I left. I never sat down and explained why that day happened, and just like I regret bringing this book out and putting her through the memories, I regret not telling her this.

I can see now that part of the reason why I can't move on and look forward instead of constantly looking back is because I never told her everything.

"I wrote that day too, Kay. When you walked out and didn't look back the way you always did...what I always knew meant you'd be back again tomorrow, it broke something in me. I knew deep down I'd never see you again, at least not the same way I had been. So I did what I always did when things hurt. I wrote."

Do I even want to know what she wrote? Am I really ready to face what happened the day I left?

For all the ways I say I'm making up for eight years apart; that I'm ready to face all of my mistakes, my demons, and other general craziness that came during a good portion of my childhood, the idea of hearing her words from that time has me wanting to admit that I'm too damn weak.

That this is something I can't handle.

For once, looking forward seems easy.

"Do you want to read what you wrote?"

"Not really." She answers weakly. "But since I'm pretty sure you didn't want to relive that day either, but did anyway, I think maybe we need to."

We.

She didn't say *I* the way I would have. She doesn't look at anything that way anymore. It's always just the two of us. A team. Partners. Neither one of us having to face anything alone ever again.

No matter what some journal says.

Where I expect her to stand and run off to our room for the journal we'd left there the last time we read from it, she doesn't. Turning even more into me instead, her lips part and the words slowly begin to fall.

Jesus. She memorized her words.

"There are a lot of people that express their feelings through their eyes because they don't have the means or ability to be able to do it in speech or even with words being written down. Kayden is a lot like that, though if you ever asked him, I'm sure he'd tell you that you're full of it and don't know what you're talking about. I saw the effect of those expressive eyes today when after walking back into the room after running off to get a drink from the kitchen, he caught my mom talking to me. His entire affect changed. Most days there's a light in his eyes, especially when he's looking at me. He's really pretty when he looks at me and his green orbs flicker and dance from one part of me to the other. Sometimes even going deeper onto his face when he changes shades of color from pale peach to a light shade of red. That did happen today, it changed, but not in the familiar way I've spent years getting used to and memorizing so I never forget. Today it was cold. Distant. I watched in frozen silence as the air was sucked from his lungs first after hearing his mom's name, and then the flicker evaporating altogether as his body went hard and ice cold."

"Belle..." I interrupt, for the first time since we reconnected, hating the descriptive power of her words. Both spoken and written. I can actually visualize the ways in which I changed that day and it's beginning to turn me inside out.

"He cursed, which he hardly ever does when anyone is around to hear, using the f word so easily. Aiming his venom at my mom first, and then, when I thought he was done, doing the same to me. Saving the best for last when mom finally left the room and he told me that he hated my stupid guts. Grabbing his bag and his coat and running from the room before I could find some way to respond. Running from me. I begged him to turn around, screamed it, but the sound didn't come. It was all in my head. Kayden, though, he's always heard me before so I knew he could hear me this time. He's the only one that can. But he didn't turn. He didn't look back. His lips didn't lift crooked like always, and he didn't so much as breathe in my direction. He was just there one minute, gone the next. Kay-Kay is just gone."

Pulling back from her on the sofa and putting some distance between us, I groan and run a hand down hard over my face before finally shifting my attention back to hers.

"Enough, Belle. I've heard enough." *Except, it's not. Not really.* "Why did you memorize this? Why not memorize the good entries? Why one of the worst ones?"

"Because it wasn't one of the worst, Kayden."

Stomach meet floor.

I already knew this, but shit. Having it shoved in my face like this? Not a fan.

"I memorized it because I spent years trying to figure it out. I needed to make sense of what happened that day and I couldn't let it go until I did."

And until now, she never had.

"How much more?" I choke out, needing to know how much longer the torture is going to last.

"Not much." She gives up easily, bridging the space between us as she pulls herself over to my end of the sofa and does exactly what I'd just planned on when it was over.

Holds me.

Keeps me close.

Never let's go.

"I don't understand why he had to leave. I know that things at home are really hard right now and that he misses his mom so much. I've caught him crying a couple of times when he doesn't think anyone else is around. I know he wants her back, and I wish more than anything I could sneak away and go find her for him. Bring her home just so I could see him smile again. But I can't, and it hurts. I can't tell him how much because he'd just feel even worse and I only ever want Kayden happy. I'm weird enough for the both of us."

"You're not weird."

"Says you. You're bias."

"If bias means, in love, then yes. Very, very bias."

In a moment that is drenched in history and pain, it's a sound I wasn't expecting to hear, but one that lifts my spirits and gives me just the right jolt of strength in order to get through it.

Her laugh enough to break through even the darkest haze.

How many years did I live without that sound? How many years am I going to spend now making sure I never lose it again?

"I want him to come back." She begins again after patting my hand. "I want him to realize what he left behind, come back and let me do what I should have been doing all this time. The thing that I only ever want to do with him. No one else. I want him to come back so I can hold him, tell him that he's always going to be my Kay-Kay, and we'll get through it the same way we get through everything else. Together. I don't think this time he is coming back, though. I just hope he realizes that when he left, he didn't do it empty handed. He took my heart with him. Maybe one day when we're bigger and he's not so mad at me anymore, he'll give it back."

"Belle," I swipe at my eye before the bubble of emotion bursts and makes itself apparent on my face. "Don't."

"Don't what, Kayden?"

"Don't ever ask me to give it back."

"I won't." she smiles before pressing her lips to the edge of mine. "But only if you promise me that you'll never ask me to return yours."

"It's stupid," I start, and when she shakes her head, I laugh. "Okay, maybe not stupid, but silly, I guess. When I walked out on you that day, when I swore that I was done and I wanted nothing to do with you ever again because you were no better than anyone else...I knew."

"Knew what?"

"I knew it would be safe with you. Which is why I left it behind."

The more I let it sink in, the less silly it seems. In fact, I'm pretty sure it's right. I walked out on her that day, but I left my heart behind. Never loving another person after her. Not girlfriends, not friends. Nothing and nobody. And I did it because if there was anyone in the world that would protect it, keep it safe and secure, I knew it was her. Even if ten year old Kayden needed a few kicks in the head for not realizing it sooner.

She held onto it until I could come back years later and give it to her all over again.

The right way this time.

There's something else I'm realizing though.

Something bigger and more important than the end result of that day years ago.

"It was never my mom, Belle."

Running a finger down across my face and along my jaw until I give into the feel of her touch and turn toward her, she smiles up at me, questions filling her eyes.

"Why I couldn't stand anyone calling me Kay or even Kay-Kay. It was never her. I made myself believe that because it was easier somehow, but it wasn't her at all. I should have realized it senior year when you called me Kay, but I couldn't stand anyone else doing it and like an idiot I didn't. It was you."

"Kay..."

"Only you, Belle. I only ever want to be Kay for you."

Chapter Fifteen

"September first, two thousand nine."

Doing a quick scan of the first couple of lines to the entry, I feel the walls beginning to close in. For every mention of Belle, there's just as much mention of Dean. None of it good. Each entry worse than the last.

Looks like Dean is taking another shot at bat.

"Uh, Belle. Maybe this wasn't such a good idea."

Glancing quickly from me down to the book, she frowns once she takes in the same couple of lines I did.

"Would it make it easier if I took over for you? Maybe read it silently?"

I love her for wanting to make things easier, but now that I know what's there, I don't think I'm going to be able to settle at all until it's done.

Just like I haven't been able to with the other entries.

Shifting the book more into my lap than hers, I silently tell her with a shake of my head that I've got this. Looking down at the page, I swallow hard, take a deep breath and start.

"I should have known when I got home and he was ten fucking sheets to the wind that the night was going to end badly. He may as well have flashed a high beam in my eyes with the gigantic sign of things to come there when he told me to drink up. It was an idiotic move, but I did it just like he wanted me to. I always do what he tells me. I keep hoping if I do everything he wants without complaining about it, he'll stop hurting me. Hasn't happened yet though."

"Breathe, Kay." Belle whispers, giving my arm a gentle squeeze. "You're already halfway there."

Really? What entry is she reading along with? All I see is a blur of lines on the page filled with my ramblings. Ones that even with the cloud that's taking over my vision, are filled with nothing but pain and heartbreak.

Lack of understanding for why things had to be the way they were.

"I got in a fight today at school. Smashed some idiots MP3 player and laughed when he cried. I expected them to call Dean. I even expected to get home and be forced under the scalding spray of the shower again or maybe some bleach in any open cuts I still had from the last time he attacked me. Not him telling me to drink shot after shot of some of the strongest vodka I've ever had. Stealing a sip here and there from the bottle he keeps stashed under his bed is one thing, but ten shots in a row with the promise of more after he goes out and gets another bottle? It's sick. Wrong."

"I've thrown up twice already." I continue, the familiar feel of acid lifting in my chest a healthy reminder of the day. *"I didn't even make it to the toilet the second time. It's all over the carpet in the hall, and no matter how much I take sponges and the mop to it so it's clean when he gets back, it won't go away. I can smell it. See the chunks. Feel the burn of another round as it threatens to come back up again for round three."*

A brush of air as it passes by alerts me to the change in the room. Belle no longer sitting beside me, but instead rushing down the hall faster than I think she's moved in years. The bathroom door slamming off the wall as she pushes her way into the room with the sound of her retching following quickly after.

This is exactly why I didn't want to do this with her. I knew she was going to react to what I'd been through.

Moving the book off my lap, I stand, but before I can even get a step or two away from the sofa, she's coming back down the hall, her expression grim, wiping at her lips and refusing to meet my eyes.

The same way she used to when I tortured her at school.

Great.

Instead of making her way over to me, she makes a beeline for the closet and after a bit of shuffling around, pulls her boots out, yanking her jacket off the hanger and slipping it on before turning back and doing the same to mine. Tossing it over to me and going back to grab my shoes. Finally meeting my eyes when I've taken them from her and slipped them on.

"What's going on? What are you doing?"

"I'm pressing pause, Kayden."

"What does that mean? And why are you putting your jacket on?"

"This isn't finished, but when you read the rest of whatever is in there, you're going to do it in front of the person that deserves to hear it."

Person that deserves to hear it.

Doesn't take a rocket scientist to realize she's talking about Dean.

"Baby, we can't just show up there. We've got to plan ahead."

Slipping her cell phone out of the back of her jeans, she tosses it to me with an indifferent expression on her face. At least there's indifference until I can see her eyes. The pools of blue sadness completely giving away her real feelings.

"Then call Tom and set it up. We're going there."

Turning her back, she takes the couple of steps to the door and pulls it open, stepping out and making sure to slam it closed behind her. Following her to the window, I see her kneeling on the grass outside, curling into herself and again, it doesn't take a genius to figure out what she's doing or why.

The entry I was reading, it got the best of her, and now she's getting the result of the overload of emotion out. It's only when her hands come up to her head and she begins hitting that I've got the door open and I'm running toward her. Grabbing a hold of her and blocking her hands from reaching their target for round two.

It's been months since she fell apart like this. When loss of control of her emotions made her deviate back to the way she'd done things in the past. Even longer since my touch alone wasn't enough to bring her out of it.

"It's okay, baby. I've got you." I whisper soothingly and as she fights against the grip I've got on her, I just hold on tighter. Refusing to let her hurt herself over something I'd already hurt enough over for the both of us. Unable to live with being the cause of her injuring herself if one of the hits she wanted to do actually hit its mark.

"I'll call Tom, Belle. We'll go right now. We'll end this, I swear to you."

As her body collapses against mine after a few more minutes of struggling, I release the breaths I've been holding in. Falling to the ground and cradling her to me and rubbing her back until I can not only feel her breathing begin to even out, but hear it as well.

"He—He needs to k-know, Kayden."

"And he will. I promise you. He will." I assure her, even though the idea of going back to Donwood Correctional isn't at all appealing. Seeing Dean again, especially right now when the wound is raw and exposed again, the last thing I want to do.

Wiping at her face, ridding herself of the tears that despite the level of calm that's seemed to take over the moment, are still falling, she sniffles before looking up.

"How many shots, Kayden?"

"Twenty-seven."

"And what happened after the last one?"

"Rick called an ambulance because I passed out in my own puke."

"Dean didn't do it?"

Son of a bitch. I don't want to answer this. I know it's only going to make a bad situation worse.

Fuck!

Sometimes I really wish I could lie to her.

"No. He just went off and drank more. Rachel, Rick's wife, rode with me to the hospital."

"I think I'm gonna be sick again." She moans, pulling out of my arms and crawling across the grass, dry heaving and making the guilt pooling in the pit of my stomach even heavier.

I did this to her.

Again.

"Kay?"

"Yeah?"

Wiping at her knees, she stands and walks back over to where I'm still sitting, the sheer level of hatred I have for what I've caused tonight making it impossible to move even if I wanted to.

What Belle is having no part of when she holds her hand out between us for me to take, not so much as twitching until I've done what she wants and slipped mine in and pulled myself up.

"This, the nightmare he's been holding over you. It ends tonight. Even if I have to be the one to do it."

✱✱✱✱✱

After a call to Tom that consisted of me basically begging him to do this, and the time it took for the man to put together the gateway needed to get us into the prison to see Dean, we were off.

The drive there a silent one, but thankfully after the excitement at home, also an uneventful one. Belle and I content to stay inside the confines of our own thoughts. The need for words in order to fill the empty space non-existent.

At least until I pull into the parking lot and she became aware of just how real this was about to get.

"Are you sure you want to do this, Belle? I can turn the car around, tell Tom thanks, but no thanks, and we can go back home. Watch a movie or something." I offer up for good measure. One that falls flat the second she shakes her head.

"No, Kayden. I'm sorry, but I've been looking over what you wrote the day after and this…it needs to happen now."

"Okay then. Let's get this over with."

Exiting the car, she slides right into place beside me as we walk to where we need to be. What I know will be the cold, devoid of life and color room with my brother waiting.

Just like last time.

Slipping my hand into hers and squeezing, I offer up as much support as I can, given my aversion to being here and it doesn't take her long to return the favor with a squeeze of her own.

As we're greeted by Tom and lead through to where we'll be meeting Dean, I realize that going into this meeting right now, she knows more than I do. She's read what I still haven't been able to open the book back up and look at. Putting me at a clear disadvantage even though I'd lived through it.

"You ready?" Tom asks, pulling us both from our thoughts and when we nod, he knocks twice on the steel door and moves back, letting me go first when it finally pulls back and we're granted access inside. Belle reaching out at the last second and resting her hand on my arm, pausing me before I can make it all the way in.

"Let me go first. This was my idea."

Moving out of the way and letting her step through, but keeping my hand securely wrapped in hers, I follow her in, only taking a seat when Belle drops the book on the table after opening it to the entry we'd left off on at home and slid it over toward my brother.

"How'd I know it wouldn't be Tom on the other side of the table?' Dean smirks and despite my desire to reach across the table and make him eat every word he just spoke, I shift my attention away and focus on the journal instead.

"Shut up." Belle says as she pulls her chair closer to the table, her hand hitting the top of the book as she shoves it so close to my brother there's no escaping it.

"You're feisty tonight. Seems like Kayden lit a nice fire up under your ass."

"Dean." I cut in, but Belle's hand coming up stops me cold.

"The last time I was here, I actually felt bad for you. When you asked me to take care of your brother, I thought I was finally witnessing the human side to Dean Walker. Turns out, I was wrong. Monsters; real ones, they don't have human sides. They're just vile all the way through."

Bringing a hand to his face, Dean fake yawns and it takes every bit of restraint I have not to dive across the table and end this for real. In the only way that would make it permanent.

"Is there a question in there somewhere? Something I can actually answer? Or did you just come here to remind me what a sick prick I am?" Dean spits out and Belle doesn't waste a second.

She's on her feet, leaning across the table until her entire hand is slamming down on the paper directly under his nose.

"Read it." She demands and despite the seriousness of the situation, there's no denying the way my body reacts to her command. How incredibly hot it is to see the girl I love taking control.

She's changed so much, but in the best fucking way.

"Story-time was an hour ago, princess," Dean sneers. "Or did you not get the memo?"

"You've never read a story like this one, though, Dean. It's a real page turner. Endless amounts of pain, agony and torture. Those are your favorite things, aren't they?"

This is the side of Belle that I always knew was there, but spent a good part of my existence trying to keep down. Even when she couldn't speak, you could see the fight she had in her eyes. Getting to witness it now, especially aimed at my brother on my behalf, well, there's nothing quite like it.

"You sold me, sweetheart." He laughs before lowering his eyes away from her and focusing on the book. Swallowing hard as I watch his eyes filter back and forth from one page to the next, the acid from earlier swirling in my stomach when he finally finishes and turns the page.

"Feel free to read the next page out loud. That's the best part."

Dean has never backed down from anything or anyone. Not when I was a kid, and definitely not as I got older. Even if in the end it was the stupidest decision he ever made and he lived to regret it, which after a lot of the fights he got into that were with bigger people than me, he definitely did, he never bowed down to anyone.

Which is why it shocks the hell out of me when he does what Belle says and starts reading.

Dear Dean,

I don't know what I did to make you so mad at me.
Maybe it was because you think it's my fault Mom left.
That I cried too much.
Cared too much.
Maybe it's not Mom leaving at all, but you ending up with me as a brother that makes you hate me.
Maybe you really wanted to be on your own.
Have Mom and Dad all to yourself.
Whatever the reason is, I really wish you didn't.
I wish that things could be the way they were when I was four.
When you would come into my room, see me playing with the Matchbox and Hot Wheels and get down there with me making up fake car crashes.
The way you would make the noises of the rescue vehicles when I drove them and laugh afterwards. Or the way you used to sneak videos into my room when I was five and let me sit with you and watch all the scary movies mom always said I wasn't allowed to see.
Most of all, I wish that things could be the way they were the first time Dad tried hitting me.
When you came flying down the hall and jumped on him. Beating on him as hard as you could with your hands until he let me go and I could get back to my room where it was safe.
I miss the way things were when you were pretending.
Reality really sucks because I love you. You're the best, most amazing big brother in the world. When my teacher asked me who I idolized and wanted to be like when I was older, it wasn't our dad I said. It was you.
I wanna be you, Dean.
I want to be the pretender.
I hate when you hit me. I hate when you pour bleach into my cuts trying to get them clean, and how you laugh when I cry. But most of all, I hate that no matter how much I do for you, nothing ever makes you happy.
I hate that I can't be good enough for you.
That I can't be good enough for anyone.

Not Mom, not Dad. Not even for Belle.

You're right.

I am worthless and it is my fault she left. But now that I've admitted it, do you think you can stop being angry so maybe we can hang out again?

I really miss hanging out.

When you read this, please don't be mad. I just wanted you to know.

I love you, Dean.

Your little brother forever,
Kayden.

"You made the boy that looked up to you, loved you even though you weren't worthy of a second of it, drink until he almost killed himself. You poured bleach into open wounds to the point where even now, he's got scars. You beat him, you used him, and you tried to kill him." Belle begins once Dean has pulled his eyes up from the journal. "But he survived."

All traces of his cockiness is gone now. His face a blank slate showing no emotion. Belle's words along with my own obviously having the desired effect and silencing him for the first time in his life.

"You beat him and bent him, but Dean...you didn't break him."

"Why?" he finally asks when after Belle's final words, the room is blanketed in silence. "Why the fuck did you bring this here? Want me to read it? What is this?"

"I wanted you to know just who it was you were torturing every time you put your hands on him. But most of all, I wanted you to know because when we walk out of here today, it's done. We're done with you and every unspeakable horror you put Kayden through. You on the other hand, have nothing but time to think. So, we're shifting the pain where it belongs. On you."

"You think you know everything don't you, little girl? You don't know shit! Your precious boy over there, he was as deep into all of it as I was. He's as guilty as I am."

Dean's barely got the words out before Belle is moving, shoving the chair back across the floor with a squeal from the force behind her body as she takes off around and right up in my brother's face. As I get to my feet in order to stop her, the exact moment the guard in the corner of the room moves the same way, Dean is falling backwards.

His chair slamming back hard against the cement. His body hitting with a resounding thud as the air is completely drained from his lungs, a muffled moan the only sound heard as the vibration from the impact of the chair begins to fade away.

Reaching out quickly and grabbing a hold of her arm, I pull her back into me, but not fast enough to miss the words that come spitting out in response to what Dean said before she flipped him on his ass.

"No one is as guilty as you are!"

Moving her back, I release my hold on her long enough to grab the journal off the table and slipping it under my arm, turn my attention back to her. Motioning with a nod toward the door, the guard steps forward and opens it, gifting us our freedom.

Freedom that even though I didn't agree with the idea at first, Belle gave me when she demanded we come here. What she secured the second she set her sights on my brother.

Isabelle Reagan not only loved me the way I never expected to be, she also freed me.

As we pass over the threshold of the door and Belle steps out into the hallway, I turn back toward my brother. Knowing deep inside this is the last time I'll ever see him, and doing what until now I'd only deluded myself into believing I'd actually accomplished.

I let go.

"I was wrong with what I said in that letter. The person I really want to be like when I finally grow up, is me. We're done here."

Stalking from the room to where Belle stands waiting with Tom and sliding my fingers through hers as we make our way toward the exit, there's only one thought I'm left with as we make our way outside.

It's just too bad the same can't be said for the journal.
The worst is still to come.

Chapter Sixteen

September 6, 2010

She's here.

Nine years I've been going to school while she gets to sit at home and do whatever it is home schooled kids do.

Nine years I've been able to keep her my secret.

My dirty one if the last four years are any indication.

A dirty little secret that's about to get blown wide open and be thrown out for the rest of the world to fuck with.

Belle is here.

So now, not only am I a freshman at another school that if the reputation I'm coming in with is any indication, I'm going to run just like the last two, but I've also got to deal with her being in my face.

Who the fuck did I piss off to deserve this?

What makes it even worse is that not even five minutes after I got there and was jumped by Amy, she's thrown right in my face.

Strolling in the front doors, I'm met with Tim's fucking laughter first. That hyena sounding shit as he guffaws like a moron and points at whatever is going on in the middle of the sea of people that have gathered around.

What I see when I get closer is Isabelle crouched in the corner, smashing her head off the side of the wall. Her pants, like every other fucking time I've seen here in the last four years, full of piss and probably shit considering she was never at any good at controlling it. A moan or a groan louder than all of the people standing around pointing and laughing at her escaping as she shakes and keeps smashing her head. What quickly turns into a squeal the more people start congregating around pointing.

I could have ended it right there. Shoved all those stupid apes out of the way until I was down on my knees beside her the way

I've done before. Rubbing her back, reaching for her hand and soothing her the way I used to. Singing to her the way I did when she had one of these freaky fucking incidents at her house when we were kids.

Singing songs that the second anyone heard, would make me an even bigger joke than she was.

Point is, I had the power to fix it. At least, I used to. Fix her.

Do I fix it, though? No. Of course not. If I went to her, all of my secrets would be exposed, and I'll be damned if I'm gonna make the next four years hell.

Which leaves me wondering what the fuck she's even doing there.

Fuck no. I can't go there. I can't care why she's at Wexfield.

The only thing I need to care about is doing whatever it takes to make sure she doesn't fuck things up for me.

Keep her silent.

Which, short of duct taping her mouth shut for the next four years, means I've got to scare her.

Make her fear me.

Something I might be able to do if I could just stop the fucking war taking place inside me.

Jesus.

It was brutal this morning and it's only gotten worse since.

Seeing her like that on the floor and knowing I had the tools to stop it, yet standing there like a fucking jerkoff and not doing a damn thing because having Tim, Amy, Charlotte and Eve laughing at the pathetic lump on the floor was easier, has been haunting me.

Belle is haunting me.

It was easier to hate her when she wasn't all up in my shit.

Now though, I'm haunted by the past. The memories. Every fucking one of them.

What I can easily go back right now and read because it's all detailed out in here for me to see.

But I'm not that person anymore.

I'm not her friend.

I'm not the boy she remembers anymore.

I'm not even sure I'm fucking human.

Shoving her to the dirt at the park last year and telling her she smelt like a fucking shit hole before calling her a retard. Laughing when tears start spilling out of her eyes and she fell in the mud puddle and starting rocking back and forth. I've got to do better. Up my game and treat her even worse.

That's better. My heads back on straight and I know what I have to do.

I have to make her see it.

See the monster.

I've got to make her hate me.

It's the only way to keep her safe.

"Jesus Christ." I curse under my breath, closing the stupid book and whipping it across the room with a growl rivalling a caged lion. "A real fucking bang up job I did with that, huh?"

Hanging my head and throwing my hands into my hair, I yank on and pull it, consumed by every ounce of guilt and self-loathing I have. Following it up by angrily dragging my hand down over my face as I expel the world's heaviest sigh. One I'm sure is coming straight from my broken heart.

Reading this shit, it's breaking my heart the same way I did hers. I can actually feel parts of it splintering, like a piece of wood being shredded. But instead of the shards just falling bloody to the ground, they're turning around and stabbing me.

Repeatedly.

What fucking thought process went into that choice I made the first day of freshman year? What planet was I living on where I thought treating the girl like a piece of shit was the way to keep her safe?

Better yet, after everything that went down earlier between Belle and my brother, what possessed me to think diving straight into when things became even more fractured between us was the way to go?

Ugh. I just want this nightmare over with already.

I'm ready to look forward now, I swear to god.

"Kay…" she breaks through, pausing me mid pace, but where before now, I wouldn't have hesitated meeting her eyes, I can't so much as turn in the direction of her voice. Can't meet those eyes. The ones that clearly show me everything she feels because she wears everything so damn openly.

I can't bear to see what the monster coming to life again has done to them.

It's just too damn bad she's not on the same page.

Calling out to me again and huffing heavily when I don't so much as twitch in her direction, she's across the floor in a flash. Her hands on my face. Yanking me with a force I didn't even know she possessed, until I've got nowhere to look *but* at her.

"How many more?" she demands, and the cold detached sound of her normally sing song voice plunges the knife in even deeper. I'm almost afraid to look down because I don't want to see what it actually feels like to bleed out emotionally.

"More what?" I finally manage to choke out through my internal despair.

"How many more entries after this one?"

"One."

"Good." She states and I roll my eyes. Hard pressed to see anything good about the situation we now find ourselves in. "Here's what's gonna happen. I'm going to let you go, and you're going to sit. I'm going to get the book off the floor and we're gonna read it together."

No fucking way. I'm done. Walk down memory lane is finished. Over it.

"No."

"Excuse me?" she asks, surprised. "I was unaware I was giving you a choice."

What the hell?

"Belle, I can't. Please. I know this was my bright idea, but I can't do it anymore. I can't break you again."

"Of course you can't break me, Kayden. It's because you never broke me in the first place." She spits out, sounding more like me with every angry word muttered. Further proving my point.

Maybe she's right and I didn't break her, but all the shit I've written, especially after we stopped hanging out, sure has changed her. She's not the same girl anymore.

I threw her right into the fire pit and stood watch as she burned.

"Sit." She demands, pulling back and shoving her hand out toward the sofa. When I make no move to do as she's asked, she repeats herself louder, and lowering my eyes away from the stress lines beginning to appear on her face, I see just how seriously she's taking this.

She's shaking.

Moving out of my grasp as my hand comes out in an attempt to steady her, she crosses the room and falls to her knees. Reaching out, I watch as she grabs the book and pulls it back into her arms before standing and turning back to face me.

"Sit down, Kayden. You want this to be over? Let's finish it."

Let's finish it.

Please God, don't let that mean what I think it does.

Tired of the back and forth, the fight between the monster I was, and the man I'm trying to be, I give up. Give in to the absolute fear and rage that her cold words have built up and unleashed in me and before I know it, I'm stalking in her direction. Obliterating the space between us, but not so much as blinking as I make my way to her, using my size as a barrier and blocking her in. Making her back up until I can actually hear the bump as her back hits the wall.

Swinging both arms out and further caging her in, I slam them down hard on the wall above and to the side of her. Moving my head in slowly, getting close enough so she can feel my breath against her face as I speak, I don't say a word. I just glare.

Where I expect her to flinch or cower in some other way, she does the opposite. Giving back as good as she gets as she stares me down, familiar fire raging in her eyes. What happens when I push her too far.

"You promised me." I roar, slamming my fist against the wall. Falling back and turning away before she can witness the tears that are now beginning to fall. "You fucking promised you wouldn't let go!"

"And I'm not." She answers calmly, her voice never wavering. "I'm not letting go, Kay. WE ARE!"

Halted by her words and attempting to wrap my mind around them, I'm not at all prepared for the barrage of fists that come flying at me. Her hands hitting my chest, one hit after another until she's successfully put space between us. Her hands quickly falling to her side when she's gotten it, but her eyes not leaving mine.

"Reading that last entry is so that *we* can let go of all of this! Not just you, Kayden. You weren't the only one living that nightmare! Or in your pity party did you forget that little fact? I lived it too! So sit your ass down and let me let go!"

When her arm moves, I flinch, expecting another assault, but what greets me when I finally open one eye and look is the complete opposite. Her hand is up, her arm is definitely out, but not in anger or upset this time.

She's trying to end this the only way she knows how.

Meeting me halfway.

Stepping toward her, I put my hand out and just like we did in our room a couple of days ago, I press it tightly to hers. Sucking in a deep breath when I make contact. Catching and releasing my breath when just like before, she slips her fingers down between the grooves in mine and holds on tight.

"You told me to take your hand, Kay. To take it and not let go. Trust me to do that. Trust me to not let go. No matter what."

Nodding, not trusting my voice to form words, much less say them, I let her lead me over to the sofa and I finally do what she's been trying to get me to since the last entry ended.

I sit.

But more than that, I trust her to do what she said.

End this.

Chapter Seventeen

"Get in." Dean grunts toward the backseat after opening the passenger door, helping Isabelle in and slamming it shut behind him.

"What the fuck for?"

"Because I've gotta take her home and I'm not in the mood to come back for your ass."

"So because Isabelle is too retarded to figure out how to use the washroom and pisses herself at school, you're punishing me?"

"What did I tell you about that?" Dean steps into my face, familiar flames of rage in his eyes matching the scowl he's now sporting on his face. "She's not retarded, and if I hear you using that word again, the belt will be the least of your worries."

The velvety way he talks about his fucking belt should scare me into pissing my own pants, but after facing the last eight years getting used to the feel of the leather as it hits my naked skin, it holds no weight.

Just another day in the Walker house.

"Take her home, but I'm not coming. I'll fucking walk."

"In the car now, Kayden!" He rages, slamming his hand down around the thickness of my arm and forcing me up against the door. Hard. The impact to my body knocking the breath and argument straight out of me.

Pulling the door open with his free hand, he tightens his grip as he yanks me around it, throwing my body in and slamming the door shut with a cut off curse before making his way around to the driver's side and sliding in. The strangest thing happening when he gets in and settles his seatbelt across his midsection.

My demon of a brother turns to the girl in the seat beside him and he smiles. A genuine fucking smile. Familiar to me only in that I've seen him give the same look to his girlfriends over the years.

Girls that until he got bored with them, he actually seemed to give a shit about. A smile he hasn't given me since I was six.

"How you holding up?" he asks her, and that's when I cut in. It's been years since I've spent more than two seconds around this girl, but I still know more than his stupid ass. She's mute. Probably deaf now too. He's shit out luck if an answer is what he's after.

"She won't answer."

"Was I talking to you?" Dean swings around glaring. "No. I didn't think so. Mind your business."

"Whatever."

Turning his attention back to Belle, I watch as he smiles at her again, only this time, there's a slip of paper held out between them.

`

Reading whatever is on the page, Dean winks before turning his attention to the car. Bringing it to life and pulling away from the curb so fast, Belle's not the only one reaching out and hanging on the door to keep steady.

Stretching my legs out as much as I can from my position behind Belle's seat, the one now shifted all the way back and leaving me shit for room, I hit the back of her chair and catch her gasp before her head flies around and stares me down.

"What?" I snap, and that's all it takes for the fear I'm used to seeing to come back. For her head to swing back around until she's staring straight ahead.

"Kayden, you wanna be pissed, be fucking pissed, but stop taking your shit out on her. She didn't do anything wrong."

"She was born, wasn't she?" I shoot back and even from my position a few feet away I can see the anger building in him. The ass kicking I'm going to get the second Belle is home safe and he's got me alone.

Good.

"I'm gonna explain something to you, you ignorant little shit. I know the way you and all your little friends see Belle, but if you pulled your head out of your ass long enough and actually paid attention or remembered shit from when the two of you were actually fucking friends, you'd know none of this is her fault. She didn't ask for it, and she damn sure doesn't want it. She's just

forced to live with it. It's hard enough to do that without having a bunch of pricks breathing down your neck and calling you retarded and deaf. So lay the fuck off."

"You done?" I egg him on, and after he grunts and curses under his breath, he inhales deeply and starts again. Only this time, his attention and voice are lower and he's not talking to me.

What the hell is it about this girl that has my normally violent brother turning into a gigantic teddy bear? He's acting like a completely different person. I don't know whether to be confused or angry. Why does Belle get this attentiveness and I don't? What the fuck did I ever do to only be on the receiving end of his hatred?

"Has he been like this the entire time?" He asks, and when Belle nods slowly, he continues. "I'm sorry for that. It's my fault."

Holy shit! Does the way his face sinks in right now mean what I think it does? Does he actually feel bad for the monster he turned me into?

What fucking universe is this?

"The reason she has accidents, why I have to bring her home, and why she smashes her head off shit and 'freaks out' as you say at school, it's because she's autistic, jackass. She can't control any of it. Body functions, reactions to stimulation, and certain situations. It's out of her control. Grace explained it, and if you'd paid attention back when she told me, you'd know it too. Or at the very least, you'd remember."

I remember all too well. I know way more than Dean does, but since I'm just a piece of shit jackass that needs to be schooled like I'm five years old again, I'm not even gonna argue. I'll sit here and take the shit he's dishing out. It's worked well so far.

Four years and counting.

"I. Don't. Care."

"You better start caring."

Yeah right. *Look where caring got me before. I'm not fucking doing that shit ever again. The cost is too damn high.*

It's much easier to not give a shit.

"Dean, just shut up and drive."

Thankfully, that's exactly what he does, after huffing out the world's most annoyed breath. Just further proof of what I've got coming when we finally get home. My open defiance right now just making a bad situation worse.

After a few minutes of silence, I'm gripping the door as he's turning again as we pull into Belle's driveway. Laying on the horn until three short blasts hit, the door opens, and Grace comes flying down off the steps toward the car. Not stopping until she's got the passenger side door open and she's practically yanking her daughter from the seat.

"Thank you." She mumbles to Dean, and with a quick nod in response, the door is again slamming on us.

Just like that, the safety net Belle provided being in the car is going, and I'm left alone with the last person in the world I want to be.

"Dean—" I go to speak and his glare when he spins around stops me cold.

"No, Kayden. It's time to shut the fuck up now."

"Like hell I will."

"I know, Kayden. I know what you, that idiot you call a best friend, Tim, and your stupid bitch of a girlfriend did to that girl. If you're not going to smarten the fuck up with the punishment the school gives you, you'll damn sure do it when I'm finished with you."

Shivering from the impact of his words, what I know is coming when we get in the house, I do what he says and for the next two minutes—the time it takes for him to pull out of their drive and across the street into ours—I do what he wants.

My only thought when I unbuckle the belt and slide out, dragging my feet slowly behind him as we walk toward the front door, one that just adds fuel to the fire in my chest when I so much as think of the girl across the street.

I've never hated her more.

She's the reason for everything.

My mom leaving, my brother picking up where my old man left off and beating the hell out of me, and now this.

She's the reason for it all.

Fuck protecting her. Fuck keeping her safe. It's open season.

I'm going to destroy Isabelle Reagan.

Flinging myself up in bed, the sound of my own screaming out enough to bring me out of the obvious nightmare I've found myself stuck in, the last thing I'm expecting is to be surrounded by not only Belle, but our mothers too.

Hell, with the way the dream was going, the way the memory of that day ends, I half expected to wake up in the corner of my room with busted ribs, a split lip and two black eyes.

"Kayden," My mom calls out. "You okay?"

"Y-Yeah," I cough out, my dry throat burning with the force used to get the words out. "I'm good. Bad dream."

The sad look in our mother's eyes tells me they know a whole lot about my bad dreams.

Shit.

Of course Belle went to them.

In between the really sweet moments we've had, the ones where we've gotten even closer than we were, there's also been a hell of a lot of bad.

Moments where I'm clearly losing whatever touch I had with reality. Being driven more into the past and who I was then ever before.

"W—what are you doing here?"

"Today is my first day at the bank. Since I don't have a ride, Grace offered to take me. She just had to make a pit stop here first."

Looking away when I see Belle begin to move, I take the glass of water she's now holding out to me and draining it dry as she takes it back and slips onto bed beside me. Smiling weakly turning back and zeroing in on what my mom said.

"A pit stop for what?"

"I had to drop something off for Belle. Nothing important." Grace interjects. "And now that I've done that, and we've figured out you're okay and not being murdered, we'll get out of your hair."

"Thanks, Mom." Belle says, and with a soft smile and an even gentler goodbye from the both of them, they're turning on their heels and heading out, leaving the two of us alone.

"You wanna talk about it?" She asks, pulling her legs up onto the bed and stretching out before turning over toward me.

"What's to talk about? It's just more of the same."

"You dream about your mom leaving again?"

"No. It was you this time."

"What about me?"

"The day your mom got Dean to pick you up from school."

"Oh," she says, realization flooding her features and changing the color of her cheeks. This time embarrassment causing the change and twisting me up inside in the process.

The only time her cheeks are allowed to change shades is when I'm saying something sweet. Not because I've brought up something better left buried.

Damnit.

"He was clean. Sober. Still a raging lunatic, but I mean, that day he was decent. To you anyway."

"I tried to talk that day. When he was going off on you in the car, I wanted to smile so badly I thought my brain was going to explode with the force I was putting into making it happen." She laughs at the memory. "He was doing what I wanted to do."

"Tell me off?"

Nodding, she laughs and I groan loudly. I remember how snotty I was. What I put into action at school every day after that one, and it makes every part of me hurt.

"You really are over it, aren't you?"

"I don't know if I'll ever be completely over what happened, but it doesn't bother me the way it used to anymore, no. We've both come a long way since freshman year, Kay. Learned. Grown up."

"Don't you mean I have? Because from where I'm sitting, you're handling it the same way you did then."

She laughs softly again and it stumps me as to why.

What is she seeing that I'm not?

"You seem to remember things a lot differently than I do. I wasn't all that well put together, Kayden. I just handled it differently than you. It hurt like hell and I held a lot of it against you. For a long time too."

"Yet you still fell in love with me."

"Well, truthfully, I fell in love with you way before all that, but since I didn't know that at the time, yes. I fell in love with you despite it."

"I did everything in my power to bury everything that happened between us as kids. The good times, the very real feelings that were developing. I held things against you that you didn't even know about, blamed you for things that you had no control over and it made it easier to keep it all down. It was also easier to do because I never really had to see you. I could pretend. That got harder to do when you came to school. You were always there, just right on the fringe. The memories right there with you. I walked a tightrope every fucking day. I acted one way to your face and another behind closed doors. It was terrible. I struggled with wanting to keep you safe from my shit, and wanting to hate your guts because you knew so much and could expose me anytime you wanted."

"This is about that last entry, isn't it? The one that you passed out before I could read?"

"Yeah. A lot of the entries I wrote about, it was like after I wrote about them, they faded to make room for other one, so I went into them as blind as you unless I snuck a peek at the book beforehand. This last one though, I remember the day and the reason I wrote it, along with the basic gist of what I talked about. I guess in preparation for what we're going to end up reading, I'm dragging other memories along for the ride. Not so good ones."

"Nothing we read changes anything."

"I know." I say, even though I'm still on the fence whether I believe it or not. "I just need you to know that the conflict I was talking about, my need to be close to you, yet as far away as possible, is there."

"And now?" she asks softly, turning her body even more into mine and brushing her lips along the thin layer of hair resting over my heart, making me shiver before finally pressing them down so deep on my skin I'm sure they're leaving behind a permanent mark.

A mark I want more than anything.

One that will match the one she's already tattooed on my heart.

"There's no struggle anymore, Belle. No tight rope I have to walk with my feelings. I love you. I'm *in love* with you, and I'm determined to be that way forever. You're the one that I want. The one I've always wanted."

"Good." She kisses my chest again before lifting her head, smiling and doing the same to my lips before pulling away, turning over to her side of the bed and grabbing what I see when she turns back over is the notebook. Taking her time opening it to where I know the last entry rests.

"Now close your eyes, focus on that, and let me finish this chapter of our story."

"This chapter?"

"Yes, this chapter. Because Kayden, the rest of our story is still unwritten. So, let's end this chapter. Once and for all."

Chapter Eighteen

October 29, 2010

Whoever came up with this stupid holiday needs the shit kicked out of them.

No, wait. I don't mean that.

What I meant to say is, whoever thought up the idea to get a bunch of kids to dress up and parade around like cattle on display on the last school day before the holiday, needs their asses handed to them.

I thought we were over that shit when we got out of junior high. Apparently when you live in Wexfield, it never goes away.

Ever.

So not only did I start my day on the opposite end of inebriated Dean's fist, requiring two showers to rid myself of the blood—his and mine—that I ended up bathed in, but I also had to put up with my girlfriend and about seventy-five percent of the school dressed up like a bunch of freaks.

*The biggest freak of all being **her**.*

For someone that I clearly remember being scared of her own shadow half the fucking time, let alone on the one day of the year that the entire town donned masks and pretended to be the things nightmares are made of, I never expected to walk through the hall and be slammed with the sight of her joining in.

With the hell me and my friends have made of her life since she got here almost two months ago, I didn't think she'd ever join in something again.

I'd made sure of it.

Securing my place as the monster of her story early on.

But there she was, princess crown on the blonde hair flowing in waves down her back. Strapless yellow dress that from the top looked tight, but that once it reached her stomach seemed to pop out. A matching yellow jacket thing covering her arms—per school regulations—and when her eyes finally turn and meet mine when she catches me looking, makeup on her face.

She was Beauty. She was Belle.

And me?

Well, in my lack of giving a shit, dressed in my normal jeans and form fitting shirt with the familiar scowl on my face, I was the beast.

For a split second after I noticed the changes in her, I wasn't though.

I wasn't the monster I'd made her believe I was. I wasn't the piece of shit asshole that enjoyed making people's lives as miserable as mine.

For one damn second in time while I stood there, feet firmly stuck to the floor staring, I could see myself being the hero.

Her hero.

The prince to her princess.

How pathetic is that?

The girl that just last week, I told Amy belonged in kindergarten. The girl that despite the way her eyes seemed to lighten and lift when our eyes met, I'd told Tim the day before, was nothing more than a stain on humanity. A mistake that her mother should have aborted.

A girl that with just one fucking look, can see something more. Sees me.

I should have been happy when she backed up like a skittish mouse when I moved toward her. When the strangled squeak slipped past her lips when I kept coming. Her fear and the tremors her body made when she attempted to get away and was met with a locked classroom door instead. The way her head sounded when it connected with the wood of the door as she started banging it, starting to break down because like the asshole I am, I was in her personal space and she couldn't speak.

It all should have made me happy.

I was scaring the shit out of her, but this time, happy was the last thing I felt.

Which is why, like a fucking idiot, I reached out to her. My hand finding her arm, but instead of gripping it the way I had in the past when I'd shoved her out of my way in the hall, I just rested it against her skin and began to stroke gently. The softness of her skin under my callused fingers offering a different kind of feeling altogether.

Comfort.

One that for the last four years I'd done everything to distance myself from.

What I can never allow myself to feel again with the way she betrayed me five years ago.

She froze and then tensed up, which I expected considering the way it's been between us since she started going to school, but when she finally finds the strength inside herself to look up and meet my eyes, its then she does the unexpected.

Searching my eyes, she studies me before those pretty pink lips of hers part and she speaks.

The first time I've heard her in four years. Since the day I left her house when I was ten and never looked back.

"Kay-Kay."

Her name for me.

The name that after my mom heard it, had taken from her and used it. A name that with everything that happened after the first time Belle said it, I never want to hear again.

A name that in that moment though, I needed her to repeat.

"Belle..."

My voice had a mind of its own. Speaking to her when the most I'd done was talk about her for weeks.

"Kay-Kay." She'd said again as she pulled her arm out from under my touch and rested it over mine.

The feel of her so god damned familiar.

"I'm sorry." I blurted out and with a quick look around me, making sure the coast was clear, I moved in closer. This time, her body seeming to melt into mine when I pulled her into me. That's when I quickly brushed my lips against the top of her head, whispered another apology and got my head on straight. Turning and walking away before she had the chance to react.

Feeling her eyes on me even after I'd pushed through the door and headed up the stairs. A look that even though I never turned back to witness firsthand, I'm still feeling on me now, hours after it happened.

Seeing her in that fucking dress, looking the prettiest I think she's ever been, I forgot about all of the reasons we can't be friends.

I forgot about my mom, the lies and secrets between us, the bullshit at home with Dean, and all of the weird and gross shit she does.

For those few seconds in the hall, I just saw her.

Isabelle Reagan.

My best friend.

The reason I started this fucking book in the first place.

The girl that no matter how badly I treated her, still has hope in her eyes when she looks at me.

Can see what lies beneath the monster.

The part of me that after Tim knocked me into her when we were all heading down the stairs later, I made damn sure she'll never see again. Laughing along with the others when she tumbled and fell. Smirking when as we all started passing her, she met my eyes, searching for something that despite my earlier move in the hall, I could never give her.

Belle might have chosen the perfect costume for us—her the beauty and me the beast—but where even now I'm sure she's still hoping for the prince to appear, it's not meant to be.

This beast isn't good. He's a nightmare.

Her worst one.

"Say something please."

I don't know what I expect her to say. I mean, what do you say after something like we just read? Sure, it was one of the safer entries, especially with all of my back and forth, but it's also another day in a string of them after she came to Wexfield High where I was determined to make her life hell.

What do you say to something like that?

Nothing is what.

"I read this last night, Kay."

She did what?

"When?"

"After you passed out."

"I don't understand. You fell asleep first. I watched you."

Nodding in agreement, she burrows herself tighter into me, releasing a soft sigh as she starts to fill in the missing pieces.

"I did, but I woke up at around one and snuck out to read. I'm sorry. I needed to know what was there."

"I'm the one that's sorry, Belle. I should have just gotten it over with last night. Been there when you read it instead of talking myself into bed. Hell, I'm sorry for everything that happened last night."

Shifting her body, she slips her legs over mine, holding me in place on the bed as she looks up and meets my eyes head on. The pained expression or worse, the pitied one I expect to see, nowhere in sight. Only the shimmering blue I'm used to.

No sign of any damage done from what she read while I was blissfully unaware.

"When you told me that you wanted me to read the journal, I knew it wasn't going to be easy, Kayden. I knew what I was signing on for, so last night, well, if it didn't happen that way I would have been surprised. You've spent eleven years holding onto all of this. I had my mom, Tristan, and people at school like Ms. Taylor to talk to. You had no one. It makes sense that under pressure, you lose control."

"Is that what you're calling me yelling at you? Losing control?"

"No." she grins, throwing me off. "I'm calling that me breaking down your final wall. The one thing that stood between us and happily ever after."

"Was this a mistake? Pulling the book out after having reasons for putting it away in the first place. Did I mess things up?"

"How do you feel after what you just read?" she asks, resting back on the weight of her legs waiting patiently for an answer.

"Different. No, that's not right. I feel better. Is that crazy?"

Bopping me on the nose with her finger she laughs and shakes her head.

"Just like you need a lesson in what's weird, you also need one in what's crazy, Kay. I'd be worried if you didn't feel better after reading what you did."

"Why?"

"Because it was the end. I checked to make sure. You didn't write again after that day. So, even if you didn't feel better, I'd expect you to at least feel relieved."

"And how do you feel?"

"Lucky."

Surprised by her answer, I inhale deeply and cough when it gets stuck. After hitting my chest a few times and then rubbing the rawness away, I ask her again, believing that in my surprise I'd heard her wrong.

"Did you say you felt lucky?"

"Yes. That's exactly what I said."

"Why lucky?"

"You mean, besides the fact that the only reason we even have these moments to look back on so vividly is because you caught me writing in my diary, got jealous and did it too?"

Well, can't exactly argue that.

"Jokes aside, why do you feel lucky?"

"Because not only did I get to know my best friend again, maybe even better than I did the first time, but through his own words, his dreams, memories and everything we've talked about since, I've gotten to fall in love with him all over again. How many people can say they get to do that? I'm lucky."

"I think with the way you're reacting to all this, I'm the lucky one."

"Who wanted to kiss who in the rain and then locked me out of the house in order to do it?" she asks playfully, wiggling her eyebrows until I break and give her the laugh she's obviously after.

"Some crazy dude?"

"Mmhmm, sounds about right." she murmurs before leaning in and kissing me. "But I really love that crazy dude."

Waiting until she pulls back, taking the familiar scent of fruit with her and giving me the chance to think clearly, I ask her the only question that matters now. What I really need her to tell me the truth about.

"It wasn't too much for you?"

"Nothing, no matter how bad it looks or how awful it may read or feel, will ever be too much for me as long as I'm doing it with you, Kay. Life with you, loving you, it's worth every fight."

It's those words that completely null and void her earlier ones. It's that answer that makes me lucky.

The luckiest son of a bitch in the world.

Chapter Nineteen

"I need a favor."

This is not the first time he's heard me say those words over the last couple of years. It's also not going to be the last. But given how often I do it, I should be prepared for the response I get once I've said it, yet I never am.

"What'd you do now?"

That one's new.

Usually when I ask my best friend for a favor, I'm met with a gigantic ball of resistance and then a boatload of pissing and moaning.

"What makes you think I did anything?" I ask, shoving him in the arm and grinning when he flinches.

"I don't know. Let's play your greatest hits and see why I would think that." He jokes as he rights himself, leaning back against the hood of the car again. "First, there was your anniversary. You remember that night, right? I'm assuming you do since it's the night Belle swiped your V card."

Great. Exactly what I wanted to deal with after the way the last few days have gone.

My greatest hits or as I like to call them, my attempts to pull my head out of my ass.

Definitely don't need the reminder of just how often I've relied on the idiot beside me.

"Yeah, I get it. I screwed up a lot before."

"Before as in last week, you mean?"

Groaning and shaking my head, I reach out and belt him upside of his head when he starts laughing.

"I didn't screw up last week. I just wanted to surprise her."

"Right." He snickers before finally ceasing to ride me. "What do you need?"

Here goes nothing.

"I showed her the book."

Right after I met Dill, before the both of us floored the gas on our asshole transformation, or in other words, back when I still had the tiniest bit of a conscience even if I didn't show it to many people, I told him about the journaling I did when my mom left.

Given the way his family was, I figured he'd understand my need to unload all of the bullshit in my head.

Long story short, he ripped on me about it for weeks. Turning almost as bad as Dean when he sucker punched me for just asking if guys could write down their thoughts. He didn't get it, but he also didn't forget it.

So I know he remembers what I'm talking about, even if the look of confusion on his face right now says otherwise.

"Since when do you read?"

"Dill..."

"Fine." He says, lifting his hands in mock surrender. "I'll stop riding you, even if it is funny seeing the veins in your head pop."

"Ha-ha. Laugh it up."

"Well, in that case." He jokes, backing up when I shift toward him and succeeding in making me laugh. "So you finally pulled it out of the vault, huh?"

"Yeah, and just like I thought, it was a lot."

"For her or for you?"

"Both."

"So you needing my help with something now is because of everything she read?"

"Kind of."

"Stop, Kayden. You're talking my ear off with all these details you're giving. Slow down a bit, would ya?"

Nice to see having a daughter hasn't changed him. He's just as annoying as always.

"Focus, jackass."

"Okay. What do you need?"

"Do you remember when you had me waste hours stringing lights up in a public ravine that had I been caught, I could have been arrested for?"

Now it's his turn to groan. What he did for Cadence is still years later the best possible material I can come up with each and every time I call on him for help.

All things considered, with what I want him to do, he's still getting off easy.

"Not this again." He whines. "We were even the day I blew up and held that balloon for you, man. You can't keep using the same card."

"Hundreds. Of. Lights." I remind him.

"Fine. What do I have to do?"

"Play fairy-godmother again."

"Excuse me?"

"You can't possibly be this slow, Dill. I'm sure Cailyn watches Cinderella a dozen times a day."

"Wrong. Babies don't care about Disney movies."

"Maybe other babies don't, but considering what you used to call Belle, I damn well know it works different in the Murphy house."

"Do I get a wand at least?"

"If it means you'll do it, yes. I'll even sweeten the deal and supply the magic."

The magic of course being my girl's reaction to what I have planned.

"You sold me. I'm in. Now tell me exactly what it is the fairy godfather needs to do."

"Get her to Wexfield Memorial Park and let me handle the rest."

"What happens then?"

"I take her back to the beginning."

I thought when I put everything together the day I proposed that we were going back to the start. Especially with the way she gave me her answer, but I was wrong.

After the way we've spent the last few days, the only beginning worth going back to is the one that happened at the park that day when we were kids.

The first time I saw her truly happy.

Pulling himself off the car and heading around to the driver's side, he gives me a nod of acceptance before pulling the door open and attempting to slide in. It's only when I see him go out of focus that I remember the other thing I'm going to need him to do for me.

"Hey, Dill?" I call out and after a second or two with no response, the passenger side window lowers and he leans across the seat.

"Yeah?"

"Pick up a rake."

"A rake?" he stares at me incredulously. "What the fuck do I need a rake for?"

"Leaves. Lots of them."

For one night, we're going to forget the fact that we're in our twenties and are supposed to be adults. Just this once, we're going to do things differently.

We're gonna be kids again.

Chapter Twenty
Belle

October 15, 2016

Empty pages are both a blessing and a curse when it comes to this book.

By the time you get this, there will be pages torn out and crumpled into balls all over the house as I try to get the words right and fail every time.

I used to hate empty pages staring back at me. Part of me still does.

What I'm coming to learn though, is that you don't have to fear the emptiness. Those lines with nothing on them, they're not daunting or there to throw you off your game.

They exist because they're for the memories not created yet.

So instead of going back in time, staying there, and reliving not only some of the best moments of my childhood, but the worst ones, I figured for the rest of the pages, I'd fill them with the present.

What I know will be our future.

So...

Isabelle.

My air. My reason. My energy. My forever.

This is my gift to you.

The moment when the past, present and future collide.

Where we make new memories for this book and for the countless books I hope come after it. Books that unlike the journals and diaries before it, we do together.

The way we were always meant to.

So get dressed. Eat the breakfast waiting on the counter (remember...I'll know if you don't), and head out front.
Your chariot awaits.
Well, wait. Let me rephrase.
Dillon awaits.
Sorry for the cheap chariot.
I energy you, Isabelle Walker, and I'll see you soon.

Kayden

PS: I know right now you're rolling your eyes because I did it again. I called you Isabelle Walker and it hasn't happened yet. But baby, if there's one thing I've learned since the day I destroyed our garage looking for the journal that would take us back in time, it's that you were always Isabelle Walker.
Right from the very first day.
And Belle...you always will be.

He's doing it again.

The boy that even to this day swears that there isn't a romantic bone in his body, is going out of his way to prove otherwise.

I thought long and hard about my place in this story. Whether or not I would include my own thoughts about the day he made me fall in love with him all over again.

It wasn't supposed to be about me, you see. This was all Kayden. At least that's how it started.

His words. His feelings. His deepest thoughts from the moment he was old enough to write them down, straight on into the moment when it stopped. Essentially, the moment that our lives as we knew it stopped.

It was never supposed to be about me because let's face it. I've loved Kayden Walker from the moment his mother walked his freshly diapered butt into our house and put him on the play mat beside me.

Every single day. Every single minute.

It's always been Kayden.

Even in the moments when I really didn't want it to be.

The boy he was, the tormentor and even tormented guy he became, and the man that with every single day that passes, I see him growing into.

I love and have loved them all.

Kayden just needed to love them all too.

So this journey that we went on over the course of those few days, where I got to meet the boy that for so very long he kept hidden from me and the rest of the world, it was about that.

About Kayden finding his way.

It really was like he said. It was the past, present and what I know will be our future coming together.

The best and the worst parts of our time together and apart joining to tell the complete story of us.

He was also right about another thing.

I've always been Isabelle Walker.

I don't need a piece of paper or a ring spun from the finest gold or silver on my finger to know that. It just is. We just are. In a world that often times doesn't make sense, and trust me, with everything I've been through and still face, it really doesn't make sense. We do.

We make sense.

So before I go ahead and do what he told me to do forever ago and shut up, be quiet and let him show you the way he took us back to the beginning again, I think it's time that I do the other thing he mentioned in the above journal entry.

Write him back.

Chapter Twenty-One

It's not perfect, but it'll do.

Okay, so maybe I'm being a bit anal about this whole thing. Perfection doesn't exactly exist, but sue me. I still want it to be exactly right.

When it comes to Belle, nothing but the best will do.

Dillon came through and considering the time of year I chose to do this in, it actually worked out even better than I hoped. Not only did he manage to put together one gigantic pile of leaves, but he had enough to work with to do it three times over.

Add that to the blanket I found packed away in our garage, and the picnic basket I talked Grace into pulling out of storage for the purpose of this re-creation and it really is damn near perfect.

The funniest part had to be the damn soccer ball I was kicking around back then. I still had it. Thing was flatter than a pancake at IHOP, but it was like even back then, I didn't want to forget a damn thing about that day and kept it.

Bringing with it all of the memories. I could smell the air the way it was then, the dampness in it because of the rain that had fallen the day before. The green of the trees, and the grass even more vibrant years later than it was the day it happened.

I'm positive I can even smell the faint trace of my mom's perfume from back then, that's how deep into this memory I've gone.

Belle's smile, the sound of her laughter and the way her skin felt when I touched her, along with the way the wet leaves felt against my skin. The slight tingle on my arms now creating goose bumps that weren't there prior to me getting here, all just further proof of everything coming together the way I predicted it when I wrote her this morning.

For so damn long, all I wanted was to get the hell out of this town. Wexfield brought nothing but painful memories and wounds that I swore would never heal over until I left. But standing here now, surrounded by the work Dillon did, and everything I've brought to add to it, well, I don't think I ever want to leave.

This place. This park. It's been the backdrop for every good memory I can remember. I can't imagine leaving it behind.

I want it to be here for every memory that comes next.

I want to marry Belle here.

Bring our kids here to play.

I want to take the soccer ball I had that day, inflate it and kick it around the grass with my son the same way that I did then. Then I want his sister to interrupt and throw him into a pile of leaves, giggling like her mother did to me.

I want all of that because it's in those moments I'll be reminded of what true love really is.

What it has the power to overcome. Change.

I'm a lot like that soccer ball.

Flattened, drained and done until she breathed new life into me.

Until she brought me home.

Home isn't a house. It's not a bunch of material possessions, like the furniture and things we bought to make what was already there better.

It's none of those things.

Home is the strong beat of a heart when you open your eyes in the morning. It's the wistful smile across the room, or the reddened cheeks of a blush when something sweet is said. It's dancing like no one is watching. It's the full feeling you experience when you're caught in an embrace. The tingle and warmth of two sets of lips touching.

Belle is home.

She's where I want to stay forever.

It was never Wexfield. It was Belle.

"Kayden," a gasp falls, and turning toward it, I'm met with the startled eyes of not only Grace, but my mom. Both of them taking in their surroundings and exactly what it means.

Their reason for being here now made clear.

"How does it look?"

"Like we went back in time." My mom says, waving her hand around. "She's going to love it."

"You think?"

Where I expect my mom to answer, Grace does instead. Stepping forward, her hand finding my shoulder and squeezing, she gives me everything I need.

"I don't think, Kayden. I *know* she will."

Looking away and wiping at her eye, I hear her sniffle lightly before she lifts her eyes again. "I always knew it would be you."

"What do you mean?"

"People were tolerant of Belle when she was younger. They wouldn't have gotten past the threshold of the house if they weren't, but it was harder with kids because what an adult might understand after a bit of explanation, you couldn't expect with a child. So whenever children besides Tristan would come over to the house, it was always a worry whether they could handle her differences. With you, I never had that worry. From the moment you were old enough to comprehend the most basic things, you were with her. By her side. Caring for her almost as much as I did. Even a time or two helping me when things were especially rough. So Kayden, what I mean when I say that I always knew it would be you, is exactly that. I always knew that you would be her soft place to land. Even when you didn't."

Grace and I have had our issues, a lot of them stemming from the years I was so lost in my own shit I stopped caring about the girl I loved, but now, with the softened yet serious look in her eyes, what she's saying, I know she means every word of. She really does believe just like Belle does that it was always meant to be us and I'm honored.

Honored that she trusted me with Belle, even when I didn't trust myself. And if I could just get past this stupid ass lump in my throat that hearing her words has caused, I would tell her exactly that.

But I can't.

With her next words, though, I start to believe I don't have to. Maybe she already knows.

"Thank you for making all of her dreams come true."

✶✶✶✶✶

What is this?

Why is she walking toward me not dressed in her normal way, but like she just stepped out of a magazine?

A ripped from the pages, real life princess.

"Surprise!" Dillon yells across the field and pulling my eyes off Belle just for a second, I give him the finger, which with the shake of his head and the returned hand gesture, is pretty evident he's caught even from his distance away.

Stalking toward her, making quick work of the distance that even with the speed that she's walking, is still too much for me, I reach my hand out when I'm close enough and take hold of hers, pulling her to me.

Making sure to breathe her in before pulling back and questioning what this is all about.

Belle has always been a vision to me. A sight to behold. The most beautiful girl in the room—the only girl in the room if we're being honest—but this, the way she looks standing in front of me now, the way the dress she's wearing seems to brush against every exposed part of my skin, she's something else.

She's Beauty.

Looks like I'm not the only one bringing memories from our past into the present.

Only hers, she's making it better than it was before.

Belle standing here in her bright yellow dress with the shimmering jewellery to match, is giving me something I never thought I'd have again. A chance to do things over. Do it the way it should have been done.

At least, that's what I hope.

"Is this what you wear around the house when I go to work?" I joke, fingering the material where it expands at her waist and meeting her eyes.

"Of course. With all the times you've called me a princess, I figured why not start living it?" she beams.

"Seriously, Belle. What is this?"

"You first." She says, moving around and taking in everything I've put together. Her eyes seeming to expand out and take in the entire park quickly before coming to land at last on our mom's sitting together under the tree. A sight that when she takes it in, she rewards me for with a soft laugh and what feels like a permanent rise to her face.

"You know what, Kay. I think I see what's going on here."

Turning back she steps back to me, her hand easily finding and sliding into mine as she turns her attention to what's laid out in front of us. Not another word, or even an idea of what she's thinking spoken.

When she stops near to our parents, I take the quiet opening I'm being given and take it.

"What exactly is it you think is going on?"

"We're starting over." She answers simply and I let it sink in. Sure, I was recreating a memory we've already had, but she's right. These memories are new because we are starting over.

"Is that what the dress is about?"

"Yes and no." she laughs softly. Fingering the dress in her hands and smiling when she catches my eyes following her movements, she meets my gaze and gives me a little bit more.

"After we went to bed, you fell asleep and I read the last entry, it got me thinking. There was something that even after everything that happened after we read it that wouldn't let me go. So I stayed awake until I made sense of it."

"Made sense of what, exactly? What a jerk I was?"

"The opposite, actually. I know what was really going on with you that day in the hall now, Kayden. Deeper than what your journal showed me."

"Okay, I have no clue what you're talking about. I'm pretty sure there was no deeper meaning. Well, other than me being at war with myself."

"Ahh, but see. There it is. You were at war with yourself, and I don't think it was just because you missed our closeness or our friendship. I think there was more to it. Another war going on that at the time, you would never admit to, but one that now, after everything I've read and we've lived through together, is clear as day."

"Tell me." I quietly push. "What can you see that I can't?"

"I see what you really wanted that day."

Huh?

"You mean me wanting my best friend?"

"Close."

"Belle," I sigh in desperation. Needing her to tell me what all of this means and put me out of my confused misery. "Tell me."

"What do you see when you look at me?"

"Right now or always?"

"Just right now."

She has no clue just how much I see looking at her. How things that shouldn't be seen to the naked eye are alive and can be seen with crystal clear clarity. Forces that have no tangible look to most people, but that are vibrant and in motion with me.

Just like us.

Our energy.

"I see the air. It cracks and sparks like flames in a fire, but the more I see of you, the more electric it seems to become. Bigger. More powerful, like fireworks on the fourth of July, but without the sound because noise...it settles whenever you're near. The only sound I can make out, the beat of your heart moving in sync with mine. Our sound. One so strong it can block out all others. Belle, you really are energy. Motion. The air."

"Okay..." she says, her voice so low it's barely a whisper, but one that despite its quiet tone, I hear loud and clear. "That wasn't what I expected."

"Now you know how I feel."

Studying me, her brows scrunching as she tries to make sense of what I've said, I step even closer, twirling a tendril of her hair around my finger and sigh as the feel of it tickles and then embeds itself on my skin.

"You weren't what I expected. Not when we were little, not when we grew up, and definitely not now. You're not at all what I expected, but you are everything I want. I want the unexpected. Love it."

Please read between the lines. Feel what I'm trying to tell you. I silently plead as seconds pass with the two of us just staring.

"I love you too, Kayden."

Thank God.

"Not nearly as much as I love you, Belle, but if you want the chance to prove you love me more, you can start by telling me why you asked me that."

"Because your answer to that question was going to lead into my next one."

"Which is?"

"With me standing here in front of you, dressed the way I am right now, recreating a memory that I honestly think we see so differently, is there anything you want to do?"

Oh, there's a hell of a lot I want to do with her. To her. I'm just not sure a lot of it is appropriate with our mothers sitting a few feet away.

"Dance with you."

"Anything else?"

"Hold you."

"Well, since you can hold me while we dance, they're the same thing. Is there anything else?"

"Kiss you."

There's a glimmer of something in her eyes, a split second where she seems to come to life, and I commit it to memory because something tells me, in the answer I've just given, I'll find the answers to exactly what this is about. What she's really doing here dressed this way.

"God, Belle. I really wanted to kiss you." I admit. My breath catching when her lips twitch and lift, confirming what I should have known all along.

What she already figured out, but she needed me to learn on my own.

Belle is giving me the chance to do what I wanted to do that day. What I *should* have done then and shit, what I'm going to shut up thinking about right now and just do.

With my hand reaching out and connecting to her face, rubbing against her skin, committing the feel of her to memory the way I've done before, I lean in and gently brush my lips across hers. Only pressing for more when her tongue manages to snake out over her bottom lip. With the park fading to black, our family ceasing to exist, and only the beat of our hearts to guide us, I give myself up to the taste of her.

The distraction she presented enough to leave me open and vulnerable as the rest of the world faded away and only she remained. Hit with a healthy dose of shock as the first blast of wetness hits me. A surprise that after I jump out of my skin is quickly followed up by the sound of Belle's laughter as more of it rains down around us.

Pulling myself from the daze that kissing Belle created, I look myself over and that's when I see what happened.

Not only did she take me by surprise showing up here this way, but she'd also taken my idea, flipped it on its head and made it her own.

Looking from my shirt now covered in wet leaves, to the still laughing, blue eyed dancing face of my fiancée, I turn as a shadow moves and that's when it all becomes clear.

Dillon switched teams.

Asshole.

"You think this is funny, huh?" I smirk, stepping toward Belle and chuckling when she starts backing away with her hands held up. Her head shaking like she's reading my mind as her eyes plead with me not to do what I am so going to do now that I see what's going on.

I'm definitely not letting her get away with this.

Swiping the leaves off my clothes, I kneel down and grabbing as many of the fallen leaves as I can, hop back up quickly and shift my attention to her, smiling serenely.

When she bolts, I'm ready, especially after catching sight of the area she's just taken off toward. The other portion of this day and what I asked that turn coat best friend of mine to put together looking to be her final destination.

It might not have gone off the way I saw it in my head, but its damn sure going to end that way.

I'm not the one going into the leaves in this memory.

Belle is too.

Giving chase, making up the head start I'd given, I pull her into my arms, spinning her around as she squeals in laughter, losing breath with every turn. Making sure that as I drop her feet to the ground, I don't give her time to get her footing, instead using her unsteadiness to push her lightly back into the pile.

My own laughter quickly joining hers until the hard shove of something heavy hitting me throws me off my own feet and straight down in the leaves with her.

"Thanks, D!" Belle calls out and before I can mount a defense, I feel her body pressing tightly to mine before she slides over and straddles me. Leaves beginning to fall from the sky, raining down over my head and landing in my face until they're blocking my view entirely. Her laughing drowning out the sputtering I do as I attempt to swipe the cool wetness of the leaves from my face.

My only thought as our eyes finally connect when we've worn each other out trying to get the upper hand, is so simple I can't believe it didn't happen before.

This is even better than the first time.

Something tells me that life with Belle is always going to be that way.

Every day, every memory.

Every single moment better than the last.

A few days together with only a book, our memories and dreams between us and I finally get it.

Belle has always been what lies beneath the ugliest parts of me.

Only ever her.

That's not all that's clear, though.

"Look Forward." They all said and now that I am, there's only one last thing to remember as we go forward.

She's also what lies ahead.

Epilogue
6 Months Later

Between classes for my degree and working at the shop, I'm running on empty.

So when I finally pull into the driveway and put the car in park, all I'm thinking about is grabbing Belle away from whatever task she's in the middle of, taking her to bed, making love, and falling asleep with her in my arms. The best gift I can think of to give myself at the end of every long monotonous day being the feel of her body pressed to mine, the light brush of her soft hair against my skin, breathing the best kind of life into me.

A life filled with contentment. Calm.

An endless boardwalk leading into forever.

What I'm not expecting is for her to be waiting at the bar, her normally bright and smiling face, subdued and serious. A detached look in the blue eyes that on an average day seem to hold all of the happiness in the world behind them.

"What's wrong?" I ask, tossing my bag to the floor, forgoing the hook and instead making my way across the room as quickly as my legs can carry me. Taking her face in my hands and studying her, the closeness of her face to mine now only making the earlier expression even more potent.

"We need to talk."

If there's one thing I've learned in the few relationships I've had, and especially during my time with Belle, is just how scary those four words can be. Especially when as far as you're aware, things couldn't be better.

Our lives settling into an even rhythm after our day at the park months ago. Each day, no matter how little time we have together during it, spent making memories.

Capturing them in pictures and words for our next walk down memory lane.

I'm never going to have a problem talking to Belle, but I'm definitely not going to look forward to it if she's looking like someone just stepped on her heart.

All that look makes me want to do is find the asshole that did it and crush them.

"About what, baby?"

Pressing a kiss to her head, I shrug out of my jacket and lay it across the bar. Making sure as I do to bypass the papers I didn't notice in my haste to make my way to her.

"I've been doing some thinking."

Throwing my ass down onto the stool and pulling her into my lap, I reach across the bar until my finger lands in the center of the papers.

"Does it have something to do with this?"

"Yes and no."

Picking them up and pulling them toward us, I take a closer look and looking from her to the papers and back to her again, she blushes.

"Why do you have these?"

Applications. Two or three different copies. For what has to be the last thing I would ever expect Belle to do.

Become an ordained minister.

Who the hell does she want to marry?

"That's kind of what I wanted to talk to you about." She says, as her cheeks continue to change shade as her blush grows deeper.

"Well, I'm all ears. I'd love to know why my fiancée, who hasn't even given me a date to marry yet, is thinking about doing it for someone else."

"It's Mom, Kay."

This is about Grace?

Wait…

"Your mom's getting married?" I ask in disbelief. I'm aware she's been seeing someone, and according to Belle it's someone that she knew around the same time she met Belle's dad, but I had no idea that it was this serious, let alone that it was leading to marriage.

Honestly, I didn't think Grace would ever marry again.

"Uh, when did this happen?"

"A couple of weeks ago. At least that's what she told me this afternoon."

"And she wants you to marry them?"

With a quick nod, she looks down toward the papers, the faintest trace of a smile beginning to lift and erasing the more serious one I'd walked in on before. The news about her mom obviously bringing my girl back from wherever it was she'd gone in her mind.

"Do you want to do this?"

"Yeah. They've even asked Tristan to be a part of it. With the way those two seem to have become inseparable since she finally introduced them, it makes sense. She wants it to be a family affair."

Belle has come so damn far since we were kids, but even now, years later, she still has trouble with social settings. Especially when there's more than just a few close people around.

Having her officiate a wedding?

What is Grace thinking?

"Is this you trying to conquer another hurdle?"

"Yes and no. I want to do this because it's something I've never done and I want to see if I can handle it, but it's also something else. She told me she can't imagine having anyone else being there for her in that way. That when she walks down the aisle to Ethan, it's not a stranger she wants to be standing in front of, but someone she loves most. She wants me to be that person and so do I."

"When's the wedding?"

"Not for a while, but you know how I am."

That's true. Belle needs the plan, even if its years off. So it makes sense that even if the wedding isn't right around the corner, she'd want to have everything prepared for when it does.

"I guess this means I'm gonna need a suit, huh?" I ask jokingly. "Is that why you looked so lost when I came in? You were afraid of how I was gonna react to dressing up?"

Smacking me on the shoulder, she laughs. "No, Kay. That's actually the other thing I want to talk to you about."

"Okay…"

Now, I gotta admit. I'm secure in my relationship. Secure in her feelings for me and the fact that no matter what gets thrown in our path, we're gonna face it and conquer it together as a team, but I'd be lying if I wasn't also waiting for the other shoe to drop.

I guess some things won't ever change.

"Okay, well, before you tell me, just answer me one thing. Does it have to do with this wedding stuff?"

"Yes." She answers easily. "Just not my mom's."

I've been wanting to marry this girl since the day I dropped to one knee in the park, so if this has to do with our wedding and what will be our marriage, then I'm more than ready to hear it. I want to take what's already in my heart and make it legal.

"Belle, just tell me whatever it is."

Going back to the pins again, you could hear one drop in the silence that envelopes the room after I've asked her to tell me what's going on. And where I could normally look to her facial expressions or the way her body sits against mine in order to figure out exactly what could be coming, I can't this time.

She's giving nothing away.

"Belle…" I whisper against her ear, breaking the silence. "Tell me what you're thinking."

"I picked a date."

Say what?

"You mean…"

"I don't want to wait anymore, Kay."

If it didn't mean throwing her off my lap, possibly over the bar, or worse, to the floor, I'd jump the fuck up right now with the surge of adrenaline that her words just caused. Words that I knew one day would eventually come, but that I hadn't been expecting for a while. At least not until we'd made it through school.

"When?" I somehow manage to choke out, calming myself just enough to press my lips to her hair when the reality is, all I want to do is spin her around until she's pressed against the bar and kiss her until we're both left breathless.

"A year from now."

"So, you want to get married next April?" I deduce, my head swimming with details and days. "But what about your birthday?"

"That's the thing, Kay. I was thinking that we could get married *on* my birthday."

"Done."

"Really? It's that easy?"

"I would marry you right now in the middle of this kitchen if that's what you wanted. But considering we've got to turn you into a minister for another wedding, I suppose I can hold out a little longer."

Reaching into the pile of papers, she pulls out a lined sheet and holds it out, the smile she's wearing reminding me of exactly the way she'd been when I walked in earlier.

"You played me, didn't you? You were never upset."

With cheeks lifting higher and eyes dancing, she grins and gives me what I'm after.

"I totally played you, but in my defense, I never claimed to be upset. I just said we needed to talk."

"Very funny."

"I thought so too." She laughs before leaning in and brushing her lips gently over the bridge of my nose. "But now that we've talked, there's something else I need you to do."

"Name it, Wifey."

Moving her eyes to the paper between us, I take it and seeing the date at the top, am taken right back in time again.

The day that through our original beginning, we were able to craft an even better one.

"I want you to read this and tell me what you think when you're done."

"What is it?" I ask, ignoring the date and the significance of it, wanting—no, needing to hear how she sees what written on the page.

"The beginning of the next chapter."

So just like I did six months ago when I pulled the dusty old journal out of storage, I do again. I read. Making sure, despite the need to stop and tell her how much I love her, to see it through to the end the way she wants me to.

October 15, 2016

Once upon a time, in a land not so far away, there was a girl.

An extraordinary girl who had abilities that often times went unseen because they were overshadowed by things that made her stand out. Made her different from the rest. Often times, not so good things. Ones that in the end would make her stronger, but also at the same time vilify her from the rest of the people that didn't quite act the way that she did.

But one day, this not so average girl, well, she met a boy.

A boy with the most beautiful emerald colored eyes that once locked on you, pulled you straight in and despite your need and desire to be let go, never did.

Eyes that the older the boy grew, the more his hair seemed to get in the way of, but whose power never lessened.

The boy held the girl, but for every second that he did, she held him.

In her arms, in her head, and in the softest parts of her heart.

She held onto him and onto his heart so tightly because the girl knew that one day, when the waves stopped crashing into the shore and the dust settled, it would be those eyes and that heart that would be her peace.

And through that peace, the boy would and could find his way home again.

Home to her.

Home to the part of her heart that she held him so tightly in.

And he did.

You see, that boy, he eventually slayed the beast that according to him had been determined to do the same to the girl, and in the end, he saved her.
In the best way possible.
By saving himself.

Kay,
You've spent your entire life believing you were the beast of this story. The monster. But the truth is, you're the hero.
My hero.
I found love, peace and serenity in you. But most of all, I found where I belong.
With you.
So, Kayden Walker...I energy you more.

Isabelle Walker <3

Grabbing the pen from the bar, I scribble the date in as big and bold print as I can before sliding it across to her. Giving her the first part of the answer she wanted when she first asked me to read.

Isabelle Walker
April 19, 2018

Meeting her eyes when she takes in what I've written, catching the tears before they have a chance to fall down her beautiful face, I go back into the past one more time. Pulling her words from that day in the gym from their place around my heart and repeating them back. The tear that slips out, along with the lift to her lips in the moment making me fall in love all over again.

"What took you so long?"

The End

What Lies Beneath Playlist

Holding A Heart – Toby Lightman
No One – Cold
Say Anything – Tristan Prettyman
Easy To Love You – Theory of a Deadman
Dancing In The Moonlight – Toploader
Colorful – The Verve Pipe
Army – Ellie Goulding
Legacy – Eminem
The Best Is Yet To Come - Hinder
Count Me In – Early Winters
By Your Side – Faber Drive
Monster – Imagine Dragons
Kiss Me – Ed Sheeran
Love Alone Is Worth The Fight – Switchfoot
Here's To The Night – Eve 6
Count On Me – Default
I Dare You To Move – Switchfoot
Love Me Anyway – Parachute
Forever – Faber Drive

Acknowledgements

Most anyone that's reached out to me during the time period in which I started the Count On Me series, knows that they're fictional stories based in my very real reality. Count On Me existing because of my daughter Isabella Rose, and one of the follow ups in Take Me With You (Eric and Amelia's Story) pulling double duty in depicting not only life with my oldest Caleb, but also the very real struggles of my best friend and sometimes co-author Joey Reagan.

So for me, there is no bigger acknowledgement that I can give then the one to my children, Caleb, Noah, Raine and Isabella (My CNRI) and my best friend Joey because truly, without them and their experiences, which in turn have become my learning experiences, these books would not exist. These characters that I have come to love as much as I do my own family, wouldn't be as alive as they are.

So to all of you. Thank you. Thank you for loving me, for supporting me, but most of all thank you for teaching me. For proving once and for all that love really is worth the fight.

Fans, friends, family. My three favorite F's (that aren't a curse word lol). Where would I be without you? Nowhere is where. So for all of you that reach out to me about my books, share my teasers, news and posts and who never waver in your support of me. From the bottom of my very humbled and appreciative heart, thank you.

Readers. Book Buyers. Blogs. Often times, the bigger we get, the more attention we receive, we can lose sight of the people that worked tirelessly to get us where we are. The real champions of this whole crazy book releasing dream. The people that anxiously wait for the pre-order to go up from their favorite author and then spread the word when it does. The people who buy the books, read the books and then talk about the books. The people that feel the words on the page, more than just read them and carry them out into the world with them. Without all of you, there would be no me. There wouldn't be any author. So from all of us as writers and publishers, thank you.

For anyone that comes across me or my stories after the publish button has been hit on this story...Thank you for taking a chance on some random Canadian woman with a dream. I love your face and I always will, no matter what.

About the Author

Melyssa Winchester is a mother of four from Toronto, Ontario, Canada.

She's currently working on Luke Grayson's story from *Remembering Sunday*, **Ready When You Are** and the third book in the *Black & Blue* series, **Heroine.**

When she's not writing, you can find her buried under the covers with her portable DVD player, watching marathons of Supernatural and Veronica Mars. When those aren't available, she can be found curled up in a corner with her e-reader and a plethora of books, falling in love with characters written so well she deems them her book boyfriends and girlfriends.

If you want to find her, check Facebook or Twitter (@WinchesterBooks) as she may just have an addiction to both. If those don't work you can always keep up with her progress on her personal site.

Other Works by Melyssa Winchester

Count On Me Series

Count On Me
Hear Me Now
Take Me With You
All My Heart
Here & Now (w/Joey Winchester)
Unbroken

Love United Series

Holding On To Heaven
No Surrender
Wanted
Stairway to Heaven
A Light in the Dark
My Heaven (Alternate ending to Holding On To Heaven)

Before The Light Series

Hold On To Me (Michael's Story)

Absence of Light (Ryan's Story)

Black & Blue Series

Shades of Blue
Into the Blue

Standalone Titles

The Space in Between
Remembering Sunday

Coming Soon

Heroine (Black & Blue #3)
Ready When You Are (Luke Grayson's story)

www.ingramcontent.com/pod-product-compliance
Lightning Source LLC
Chambersburg PA
CBHW060819120626
46557CB00001B/278